BRIEF DESCRIPTION

The time is 1970. In the short span of ten years, a powerful new industrialization has grown up in the west of Ireland —Industrial Corporation Eire. Behind its own rigidly controlled "Iron Curtain," its scientists have solved many of the major problems with which the rest of the scientific world is still futilely grappling. The face of Ireland is being transformed, but more important to the great powers is the inherent menace these prodigies of scientific achievement may offer to the delicate balance of power in a badly divided world.

All attempts to discover the origin, nature and purpose of I.C.E. are easily thwarted by the Irish Secret Service and I.C.E.'s own Intelligence Section, until Thomas Sherwood, a young Cambridge scientist, is sent by British Intelligence to investigate. Sherwood immediately finds himself in a world of desperate violence. He is pursued across Ireland by spies and counterspies, and he tangles with still other agents who are stealing scientific information to sell to the highest bidder. His scientific abilities plus his tenacity and endurance finally bring him to a solution of the mystery.

Fred Hoyle, a world-famous astronomer, demonstrates again his versatility. *Ossian's Ride* reveals Mr. Hoyle's familiarity with western Ireland, mountain climbing, electronic computers and the writing of lively popular fiction.

OSSIAN'S RIDE

OSSIAN'S RIDE

BY FRED HOYLE

HARPER & BROTHERS   NEW YORK

CONTENTS

PROLOGUE   7
1.   PRELIMINARIES IN LONDON   10
2.   INTO ENEMY TERRITORY   17
3.   THE HOUSE IN MARROWBONE LANE   31
4.   THE MINSTREL BOY   45
5.   THE CHASE ACROSS THE COMMON   56
6.   THE JOURNEY TO THE SOUTH   68
7.   THE END OF P.S.D.   80
8.   FIRST ENCOUNTER WITH I.C.E.   88
9.   JOURNEY TO THE COAST   96
10. BEYOND THE BARRIER   110
11. THE CLIFFS OF INISHTOOSKERT   124
12. THE INDUSTRIAL CORPORATION OF EIRE   135
13. SOME INFERENCES   143
14. CAGED   148
15. CHANCE PAYS A VISIT   159
16. BREAKTHROUGH AT LAST   167
17. INISHVICKILLANE AGAIN   177
18. AT THE STRAND'S EDGE   185
EPILOGUE   189

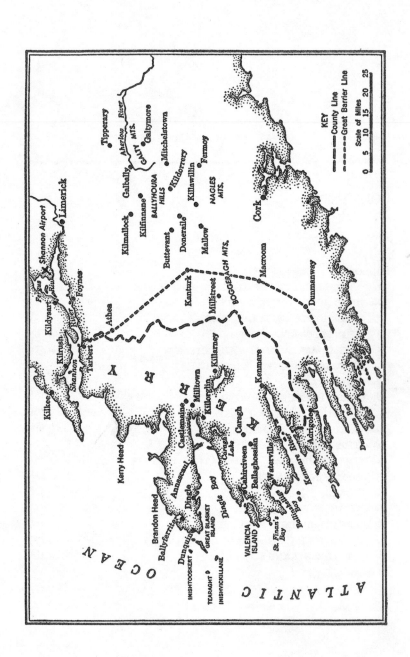

PROLOGUE

The Old Man was in a regular stew. So much had been clear to Geoffrey Holtum, his private secretary, from a short conversation over the telephone. It was a fair inference that the appalling Irish problem must have something to do with the P.M.'s state of mind. But why should the crisis be any worse in that particular direction than it had been yesterday, or last week, or last year for that matter?

Holtum knocked lightly on the sanctum door.

"Come in," boomed the Prime Minister. "Thank heaven you're back, Geoffrey," he went on, "just in time to keep me out of the clutches of the psychiatrists."

"What's happened, sir?"

"What's happened! This!" The Prime Minister brought his fist down with a thump on a large typescript that lay in front of him. Then he picked it up and brandished the pages in Holtum's face. "This damned stuff. It may be the most significant document that has ever come into my hands, or it may be just a tissue of rubbish. I simply don't know which."

"But what . . . ?"

"What is it? Nothing short of a complete explanation of the whole I.C.E. mystery. That's what it claims to be!"

"Whew! But how . . . ?"

"How did it come into my hands? Listen!"

7

Holtum wondered when he had ever done anything else but listen to the P.M.

"About a year ago, one of our Intelligence people had a brain storm, not a bad idea really. Instead of continuing to send our normal agents into Ireland, he got hold of a young chap from Cambridge, a clever fellow—science and mathematics and all that sort of stuff. Name of Thomas Sherwood, from a Devon farming family, good solid yeoman stock. I've had a very complete investigation of him carried out by Intelligence."

The Prime Minister lifted a large file, and then dropped it back again on the desk top.

"Judging from what Intelligence says, I'd swear that Sherwood is absolutely one hundred per cent reliable. Yet on his own admission he's now completely gone over to I.C.E.! Then having sold out on us, he proceeds to send me this report, which is absolutely tremendous in its implications if it happens to be true."

"Does he give any reasons, sir?"

"In heaven's name, yes! I wouldn't blame him for selling his soul to the devil, if what he says in here is true."

"But is there any conceivable motive for sending the report?"

"You know perfectly well that together with the Americans and the Russians we're now working up quite a pressure on I.C.E. If I believed in the veracity of Sherwood's report, I'd instantly recommend that this policy be scrapped forthwith."

Holtum whistled. "And so it might be a colossal bluff."

"Or it might be a warning, I don't know which."

"But surely in the course of such an extensive document it must become clear whether this man Sherwood is on the level or not."

"That's exactly what I'm going to ask you to judge for yourself, Geoffrey my boy. I've already arrived at an opinion myself, so I'm not going to say anything more that might prejudice you on the main issue. I've got an additional copy of the report. I want you to take it away. Go where you can read it quietly without interruption. And take this Intelligence stuff as well."

8

The Prime Minister handed over a couple of fat folders.

"Don't waste any time checking on the facts. I've done that already. Everything is impeccably correct. We even know that some rather peculiar people who appear in the story really do exist. We have this on the testimony of a certain internationally famous pianist, whose name I won't mention. He was invited to give a series of concerts at I.C.E., in the course of which he met, albeit rather briefly, some of the high-ups in the organization. Strange that we should have to rely on a musician for our best information. Shows what a beating our Intelligence Service has taken from these I.C.E. people.

"Remember, above all, that you're dealing with a very astute young man. Remember that he may even be adept at telling the truth in a way that gives a wholly false impression."

"You mean, sir, that it's more a question of character than of logic?"

"Exactly so. Try to get yourself into this fellow's mind. You're fairly well of an age together. You should be able to judge him better than I can."

Holtum dined at a quiet restaurant, a well-filled brief case at his side. He took a taxi to his apartment. With a large pot of fresh coffee, he pulled out the P.M.'s bundle of papers. A sip of Cointreau first, and he took up the first page.

1

PRELIMINARIES IN LONDON

From my school in Ashburton, Devon, I won a major scholarship in mathematics at Trinity College, Cambridge. I took my B.A. degree in June, 1969, specializing in my final Tripos in algebra, functional analysis and topology. This is relevant to what is to follow.

By the early summer of 1970 I was well started in research, on a problem in the theory of infinite groups. I was just turning over in my mind what I would like to do during the summer vacation when I received a curious letter from an address in Whitehall. The letter offered interesting employment for the months of July and August. The writer was wholly inexplicit, however, about the nature of the employment. No doubt I would have ignored this communication altogether had it not been for one slightly singular feature. I was informed that, if I were so minded as to accept the invitation, an appointment would be available at 1:15 P.M. sharp, on June 27. The signature was entirely illegible.

There were several things that I wanted to do in London, so I decided that nothing would be lost by finding out what manner of civil servant would fix an appointment during the lunch hour. Was a fat man on a slimming diet? So I wrote in return that I would present myself at the agreed time. I received a second letter describing the particular office I was to ask for, the signature being quite as illegible as before.

I was welcomed by a very nice-looking brunette.

"Ah, Mr. Sherwood," she said with a smile, "you are to come this way."

We walked possibly three hundred yards along a multitude of corridors, and we climbed possibly two hundred feet up and down staircases before we reached a place that looked more like a private den than a public office. A very sunburned, rubbery, bald little man of perhaps sixty motioned me to a chair. His face was weather-beaten, his temples were creased by a multitude of wrinkles and his teeth were tightly clamped on a huge meerschaum.

He puffed away for perhaps a minute, staring hard at me the while. Then he broke into a chuckle.

"Well, well, Mr. Sherwood, so you fell for the old 1:15 trick after all!"

"I'm only too glad to hear that the trick wasn't just a trivial oversight, Mr.—?"

"Parsonage, Percy Parsonage at your service."

There was a knock and the brunette came in with a tray. "Lunch for Mr. Sherwood," she explained.

"That's right, feed him," nodded Parsonage. "I won't eat myself—didn't breakfast until eleven-thirty."

I had just taken my first mouthful when he asked, "And how would you like to make a trip to Ireland?"

I swallowed carefully. "From all I hear of Ireland, a man might get himself killed a score of times a week—in your line of business, Mr. Parsonage!"

"And what would you know of my business?"

"Nothing at all. That's why it would be foolish of me to agree to go to Ireland on your behalf."

Papa Percy (as I soon learned he was called) picked up his great pipe and said, "I wouldn't have put you down as the sort of young man to turn aside at a suggestion of danger."

"That would depend on whether the danger was of my own making or not."

Thoughtfully Parsonage moved to a wall on which a large map of Ireland was hung. Prodding it, he said, "Let me show you the cordon beyond which no ordinary visitor to Ireland may penetrate, beyond which even no Irishman may pass unless he has satisfied the most rigorous security check. See how it runs, from Tarbert in the north, to Athea, south to

Kanturk, and beyond directly over the Boggeragh Mountains to Macroom and Dunmanway. See how it bends here to the sea in Dunmanus Bay."

For a moment he puffed furiously on his monstrous pipe and then went on. "Within this tight wall incredible things are happening. The main activity seems to be confined in the central peninsula of Kerry immediately to the south of Lake Caragh—where Ossian is said to have once ridden over the western mountains to the Land of Youth.

"Now, Mr. Sherwood, I would like to send you on an absolutely individual mission. The last thing I want you to do is to get mixed up with the usual espionage work, ours or anyone else's. Every nation on earth is directing ninety-five per cent of its undercover activity to Ireland. The place is simply crawling with agents. And the Irish themselves have naturally started an intense counterespionage drive."

"I don't see any niche in all this that seems specially designed for me," I said between mouthfuls.

"I sincerely hope not. Ireland is a fantastic maelstrom of intelligently organized thuggery. If you're unfortunate enough to get mixed up in it, you'll be lucky to stay alive even for a couple of days."

A chicken bone seemed to get stuck in my throat.

"Don't get impatient," said Papa Percy. "In my roundabout way I'm gradually coming to the point. Here, take a look at these."

He took three documents from a small safe and flung them down on the table at my side. The first was concerned with a bacteriological topic; the second was a plan of somethi¬g that looked superficially like a furnace. The third was mathematical in form, more in my line.

When I began reading it in detail, Parsonage roared, "Don't bother. It's arrant nonsense. Let me tell you something about this one." He picked up the first document. "It was obtained in a most desperate operation. Two of my best men were killed. Yet it contains nothing but rubbish." He strode about the room munching mightily on the meerschaum.

"You see all our ideas of intelligence work simply go by the board when we have to deal with this scientific stuff."

12

He flourished the papers. "Our men can't tell whether this is genuine or not. All they can do is fight to get hold of it, and fight they do, often dying in the process."

"So you want me to vet things. I'm not really enough of a scientist, you know."

"I want much more than that! Suppose this junk was genuine. How much would it tell us? Just a little about what was going on in there." He pointed to the wall map with his pipe.

"No, I want more than that, very much more. I'm going to give you a lecture. Don't interrupt! How much do you know about I.C.E.? Only a little, I'll warrant. None of us knows very much for that matter. I'll tell you what *I* know."

The little man made an odd sight as he marched around belching clouds of smoke, his hands behind his back.

"Pour me some coffee," he bellowed. "I.C.E., the Industrial Corporation of Eire, came into being some twelve years ago. A small group of very able scientists approached the government of Eire with what seemed an entirely straightforward proposition. Their proposal was to establish an industry for the extraction of a range of chemicals from the organic material in peat—turf, as the Irish call it. Since their initial capital was rather small, it was requested that they be allowed to plow back all profit for a period of ten years, after which normal taxes would be paid, subject to a maximum payment of five million pounds in any one year. This seemed tolerably reasonable to the Irish government, and it was accordingly agreed to.

"Within a short time, I.C.E. was producing an amazing range of valuable chemicals, ostensibly from turf as raw material, although whether this was really so is open to doubt. At British chemical concerns there were many red faces, I understand, during this phase in the history of I.C.E. Still, no one thought anything really remarkable was happening. All was to be explained in terms of the ingenuity of a few really clever fellows, fellows who intended to acquire for themselves a large slice of cake, and who were very sensibly cutting it outside the taxation laws of the United Kingdom.

"Profits increased rapidly. The Irish were regretting the terms of their agreement, when I.C.E. acquired enormous

13

local good will by voluntarily paying to the government the sum of two million pounds. This was in the fourth year, just before the coup on which the real basis of their expansion was founded."

"You mean the contraceptive pill," I remarked.

"Yes, the contraceptive pill. Just what the world's population problem needed. Sales were vast beyond precedent. By the end of the eighth year the capital resources of I.C.E. exceeded the thousand million mark."

"I've never understood how it came about that the Church didn't stop it. The contraceptive business, I mean."

"Ridicule, my boy. If I may parody the poet Schiller: Against laughter even the Hierarchy fights in vain. Think of it, contraceptives from turf! For decades the Church had fulminated against their use, while all the time, outside every cottage, there'd been piled a whole mountain of the stuff!

"As a matter of some interest, and as an indication of the perversity of mankind, the birth rate in Ireland has actually risen since the use of contraceptives became widespread there. Pour me another cup."

Parsonage swallowed the coffee at a gulp, and went on with his lecture.

"Where were we? Still six years in the past. From every point of view this was the critical stage in the development of I.C.E. The emphasis began to change from chemistry to physics. Unobtrusively, physicists and mathematicians were offered attractive positions and the number who accepted the flattering offers was not insubstantial. The volume of scientific immigrants has steadily increased and is still increasing."

"Doesn't this immigration give an ideal opportunity for finding out what's going on? By sending in a few of your own fellows I mean."

"You might well think so. Most of what little we know has come that way, but our efforts seem to disappear like rain in a desert. These people are devilishly clever. They've made very few mistakes. They seem to know just who they can trust and who they can't.

"Six years ago I.C.E. began importing metals. As I was saying, this coincided with a marked shift from the chemical to the physical side, all of which culminated a little more than a year ago in a chain of commercially working thermonuclear reactors."

I whistled in astonishment. Research in the thermonuclear field is of course a largely classified subject, so I had no precise knowledge of how things were going here in Britain, or in the United States or elsewhere. But it was an open secret that the whole business was turning out to be a pretty sticky proposition.

"How should this be possible?" I said.

Parsonage flung down his pipe with a flourish. There was a shower of sparks which I made haste to quench. "Now we come to the kernel of the whole infernal business. How was it possible? That's just what I want you to find out!" He glared at me with a fierce intensity.

"Mark my words carefully. It isn't at all that I want you to find out the technical solution of the thermonuclear business. If you do find out, well and good, but on no account must that be your main aim."

"I see through a glass darkly," I managed to interject. Parsonage fairly danced as he stood in front of me.

"See here—a man has one thousand pounds. By playing the stock markets he becomes a millionaire within five years. Don't laugh, it can be done, if you can forecast correctly just what is going to happen. That is what I.C.E. has done! See how they built this reactor! No extensive preliminary research, just a systematic manufacture of all the relevant components. Sherwood, my boy, this is the crux of the affair. How did they know beforehand so unerringly just what they were going to do? That's what I want you to find out. Don't worry your head about technical details, about secret agents, about anything other than the principle of the thing. How do they *know?*"

At last I had a glimpse of what Papa Percy was driving at.

"But why me?"

"Why not?"

As I pondered this impossible reply, he went on. "What qualifications are needed, you've got."

Something was wrong with the grammar.

"Just as a baby picks up his mother tongue, so a young

man of your age picks up information. You are highly trained in the right sort of thinking. This is a logical problem, not one of scientific or engineering detail."

He tapped the map. "The scene is set in wild country. You're a country lad; a townsman might find himself in trouble over there. What else?" As I pondered things, he stuffed great fingerfuls of tobacco into his pipe. In spite of a riotous confusion of expression, Parsonage had driven home his point.

"So what you want is the logical taproot . . ." I got no further.

"Right-right-right, ad infinitum! The taproot is what I want, the power source, the driving force. Now you have it, my boy. Don't imagine this to be one of your academic exercises. Five years ago it was an academic exercise. We could have moved our troops into Ireland then. We could have taken I.C.E. slowly apart, piece by piece. But we can't do that today, nor can the Americans or the Russkoes."

"I can't see why not, if you really don't mind being drastic."

"Think, young feller. Use your sconce-piece. When you find someone far ahead of you in one line of business, you can bet a king's ransom to a tin of fishing bait that he will also be ahead of you in other lines, avenues, byways, conduits or what you will. If I.C.E. can make a thermonuclear reactor they can make an I.C.B.M. If they can make a contraceptive pill, they can make a pill that would make us all die of laughter."

Parsonage stood before the map, legs apart, defying all laws relating to the smokeless zone.

"We can smuggle you into Ireland through the usual pipe line, or you may prefer to travel more openly. That's for you to decide. Go away for a couple of days, think about it. Need any money?"

I nodded, so he offered me a bundle of notes.

"Not so much, only about fifteen pounds. I'm not going to make myself conspicuous. I might as well begin straightaway."

There was one question I would have liked to ask, but my nerve failed. I had always understood that the main danger to an agent comes from his own people. I feared that Parsonage and his pipe might explode if I were to ask him if this were really so.

Nor did I tell him that it had been my dearest wish to get a chance to visit Ireland. I had been pondering precisely the question of whether my funds would run to such a trip when his first letter arrived.

Nor did I tell him that besides buying a few necessary articles, I also contrived with his fifteen pounds to take out the brunette from his office twice.

2

INTO ENEMY TERRITORY

I caught the 3 P.M. express from Paddington to Fishguard deliberately with only a minute or two to spare, as a precipitate young student might be expected to do. There was a vacant center seat in one of the compartments, so I heaved my rucksack onto the rack and settled down, ostensibly to read the *Times*. Behind its welcome shield I reflected on the situation.

It had been an obvious decision to try to enter Ireland in the most open manner possible. If I failed I could always fall back on Parsonage's "pipe line." If I succeeded I could go about my business with less possibility of interference from Irish counterespionage. This suggested the reflection that although still in England, the affair had already begun. For the Irish must certainly have men on the train, men who would watch and talk with the passengers, men who were trained to separate sheep from goats, which isn't after all a difficult matter. The slightest false move now could lead to disaster a few hours later when I should have run the gantlet of Irish immigration.

The visa was my chief worry. It took three months to get a genuine visa, always supposing that one were granted at all. I had been in favor of waiting, but Parsonage would hear none of it, insisting that within an hour he could supply a forgery that was entirely indistinguishable from the genuine article. No doubt this was true, but I was less sanguine about Papa Percy's ability to conjure my name at a few days' notice into the lists possessed by the immigration officials. Unless this documentary sleight of hand had been well and truly executed, I was going to be in the soup all right. The argument that had appeared so convincing in the shelter of Parsonage's room now seemed rather threadbare.

"Even if you were to wait, there is no guarantee that you would get a visa, and even if you got a visa, there is still no guarantee that you would ever get into Ireland," he had argued. "Very wisely, the Irish are managing the whole visa business with an assumed air of incredible inefficiency. This allows them to turn down, and turn out, anyone they please. It dissuades the genuine traveler, and above all makes difficult any diplomatic protest from our side."

This was the first of my two worries. Money was the second. Since Irish currency is now as "hard" as it is possible for any currency to be, I was obliged to ration myself to the very moderate official allowance. I might of course have risked carrying more, but if I was searched the game would instantly have reached an ignominious end, for any British traveler with more than the allowance of his own government in his pocket would instantly come under the gravest suspicion.

Parsonage had brushed the matter aside by insisting that, once in Ireland, I could pick up as much money as I wanted from an agent in Dublin, to wit a Mr. Seamus Colquhoun, who lived at an address in Marrowbone Lane. This arrangement was probably perfectly in order, but I had a strong feeling that the more I could keep away from such people the better I would be pleased.

These reflections seemed to about exhaust the potentialities of the *Times*, so I started a paperback written by an angry young author who had gone down from Cambridge a few years earlier, I am sorry to say from my own college. It was tough going, but I stuck determinedly at the task until the train reached Cardiff.

After Cardiff, I made my way to the lavatory at the near end of the compartment. It was locked. A voice in my ear remarked, "Funny, it's been locked every time I've come past, ever since we left Reading."

It was a ticket collector, or rather (for precision's sake) it was an individual in ticket collector's uniform. He banged hard on the lavatory door and shouted, "Hi, inside!" When after a couple of minutes of shouting and banging there was no reply, he remarked in what I took to be a commendably casual tone, "I think we'd better have that there door open."

With a tool from his pocket, the like of which I hadn't seen before, he shot back the bolt, opened the door, glanced inside and said in a slightly puzzled manner, "Bloody silly trick. There's nobody in. Can't say I see how the door got fastened.

"Ah, well, sir, it's free now," he added.

He was right; there was nobody inside. But it needed only the briefest scrutiny to see that something was very wrong, or more accurately that something had been very wrong. For here and there dark blotches were spattered over the interior of the place. I touched one, and my hand came away sticky and red.

"There's been some serious trouble," I said as I stepped back into the corridor. The ticket collector had evidently gone into the next compartment, so I crossed quickly through the connecting door. A glance down the corridor showed that in the odd second or two the fellow had vanished. My instinct was to follow quickly, but reason insisted that it was best to think first. There must be an explanation of why the ticket collector had opened the lavatory door, of why he had disappeared. I glanced down at my trousers and cursed aloud as I saw I must have brushed against one of the dark patches. Damn it, must I go bloodstained through the trickiest part of the whole business?

My first thought was to change into walking shorts. I had deliberately not dressed in outdoor clothes and boots, feeling that it would be wrong to overemphasize the student-hikes attitude. Now I would have no choice, it seemed. In a few strides I was back at my compartment. There were still three men in it (two people had left the train at Cardiff), but my rucksack had gone.

It is said that a dying man can review his past life in a second or two. Balderdash of course, but it is surprising how fast one can think when the occasion warrants. The thought exploded in my head that at all costs I must behave as an innocent young student would behave. In short I must raise the devil of a shindy. Scarcely checking my speed I opened the compartment door, looked up at the rack and said in the most surprised tone I could muster, "What's happened to my rucksack?"

Two of the men, ages perhaps thirty to thirty-five, were drowsing or pretending to drowse. The third fellow was much older, maybe fifty-five. At my question he put down a book, looked me over with questioning blue eyes and said in pronouncedly Irish speech, "But you fetched it yourself, not a moment ago."

"I did no such thing! Surely you must have seen someone come in and take it?"

"Certainly someone came in. My attention was on my book here, so I naturally took the person to be yourself. He was of about your height and coloring."

"You'd better find the guard," remarked one of the younger men.

"I'll find the guard and the police at the next stop."

The fellow was of course right, I should go at once and find the guard. But at all costs I must first have time to think.

It seemed inconceivable that my rucksack could have been stolen by anyone who knew the real purpose of my journey. Or was it inconceivable? Could my connection with Parsonage already be known to the Irish? Was there a spy in his office? Even so, the Irish would scarcely take action here on the train. Assuredly they would wait until I reached Rosslare. No, the business could have nothing personal to do with me; it must be the rucksack. Yet the rucksack contained nothing but a couple of books and my walking outfit—a good disguise for a man who had urgent need of a quick change of clothes, perhaps for a man whose present suit was liberally dappled with blood? The disguise would be useless, however, if I were to let out an enormous roar at the first glimpse of my own shirt, pants and boots. Therefore it followed that I must be hit over the head, or worse, on my way to find the guard.

It was natural that this process of reasoning should cause me to direct an overpiercing stare at the man who had suggested seeking out the guard. It was equally natural that he being taken unaware should have betrayed his complicity. There was no "sudden start," so beloved by the writers of fiction, no "sudden pallor," no "beads of perspiration." All that could be seen was a ripple of emotion that crossed the fellow's face, as fleeting as a puff of wind on a grassy meadow. Yet if a confession had been sealed, signed and delivered, the situation could not have been clearer.

Three of us leaped upward. Strong hands gripped my waist and shoulders, heaving hard to throw me to the floor. But my right hand had reached the communication cord in time, and the weight and pull of their bodies only whipped the cord down the more fiercely. Already the train brakes were on.

Quite incredibly, one of the fellows seemed to think he could bluff the matter out.

"There, look what you've done. It'll cost you five pounds." His companion had other ideas, however.

"Don't be a fool, Karl. Let's get out of here." I was too shaken to do much to stop them, but I managed to stick out a foot in time to trip Karl as he moved quickly to the door. He fell across the corridor, striking his head a resounding blow on the brass hand rail that ran along the outer window. His companion gave me a furious glance, grasped Karl firmly by the shoulder and humped him along the corridor. I decided to let them go. They were probably armed, and shortly I would be having other troubles.

The outer door was flung open and a voice shouted, "Now then, what's going on in here?"

Do the same robust elements of officialdom have no other way of approaching a crisis?

"That is very much what I would like to know," I replied.

A large guard hauled himself into the compartment. Outside there seemed to be the driver, a fireman and perhaps three or four other officials. Everywhere along the train, heads were sticking out of windows, male and female, hatted and bare, blond, white, brown and black.

"One of you must have pulled the chain," observed the guard to the Irishman and me.

"I did."

"Why? What's the matter? Everything looks all right in here."

"I pulled it on impulse."

The guard leaned out and remarked to the driver, "He says he did it on impulse."

"Impulse be b——. We're late," was the driver's view of the matter.

The guard turned heavily on me.

"Now, young man. This is a serious matter. It's going to cost you five pounds."

The thought struck me that a hundred years ago five pounds must have been quite a substantial sum. Stopping a train without good reason must then indeed have been a serious matter. But now, after a century's inflation, of what significance was five pounds to a man with a taste for entertainment?

"I did not say that my impulse was unfounded."

The Irishman decided to rescue me from further misunderstanding.

"This young gentleman has just had his rucksack stolen."

"That's no reason for pulling the chain. He could have come along and found me without stopping the train."

"There you reveal your ignorance of the matter—if I may say so. Had I tried to find you, I should unquestionably have been hit over the head—coshed, if you prefer the word—and possibly obliterated without trace."

The guard again addressed his colleague. "Better come inside, Alf. We've got a bloody lunatic to deal with."

Alf, the fireman, climbed in with considerable agility. Evidently my trump card had better be played without delay.

"Mention of blood reminds me that the lavatory nearby,

the one immediately to the left down the corridor, happens to be liberally spattered with the stuff."

"Didn't I say he was daft?" breathed the guard in stertorous fashion.

"Wouldn't it be worth while stepping along to the lavatory, just to verify my story? It will consume only a few seconds of your valuable time, and it will save Alf and me from doing serious damage to each other."

The guard responded in commendably scientific spirit.

"Oh ho," he said, "we'll soon see about that."

As he forged into the corridor, by the way that Karl and his companion had departed so hurriedly only a few moments before, it occurred to me to wonder if the stuff in the lavatory really was blood after all. Suppose it turned out to be catsup? The nearest pair of doctors would undoubtedly be only too ready to subscribe to the guard's rough-and-ready analysis of the affair. But did catsup become tacky as it dried?

A worse thought: If events were to follow the accepted pattern of the thriller or detective story, assuredly the lavatory would turn out to have been cleaned of every telltale speck. What could I do then but point out the unnatural cleanliness of the place?

My fears were groundless, however. In a trice the man was back.

"This is a serious matter," he announced. "What's been going on here?"

I decided that the fooling had lasted long enough. "Could I see your credentials, please?" I asked.

This caused him to blink rapidly for about ten seconds. Then, "My what?" he boomed.

"Your credentials, your bona fides as a member of the police force."

"I'm not in the police, you perishing lunatic."

"That's exactly the point I am delicately hinting at. Don't you think this is a job for the police? By now every criminal who was on the train must be at least a couple of counties away. Alf, you got any steam left in this old tub?"

The latter remark brought out the raw primitive in Alf.

"I'll put some steam in your bloody kisser if you don't shut up," he growled as he dropped to the ground outside. The guard banged the door shut and crossed into the corridor, where he stood truculently until we reached Swansea.

I suppose he couldn't really be blamed too much for questioning my sanity, for my story sounded quite fantastic even to my own ears when I described it to Inspector Harwood of the Swansea Police. Naturally I said nothing of the real reason for my journey to Ireland, but everything else I described as accurately as I could, exactly as it had occurred.

"Well, Mr. Sherwood, I'm afraid we shall have to ask you to remain in Swansea for a day or two until we have had the opportunity to check up on this odd business. I'm sorry to have to delay your holiday, I know how I'd feel about it myself if I were in your position, but I'm sure you'll realize that it's really absolutely necessary."

Should I ring Parsonage and ask him to get me out of this ridiculous situation? An idea occurred to me, and I decided not to be such a fool.

"Naturally, Inspector, I'm not pleased about being held up, but if that's the way it is, there's really nothing to be gained by arguing. Might I ask you to fix me a rather inexpensive place to stay at? You see I didn't bring much cash with me as I didn't expect to be here in Wales for more than an hour or two."

"There's no difficulty about that, sir. We can advance you a reasonable amount for living expenses. There's quite a tolerable bed-and-breakfast place in Cromwell Road. I'd be glad to make arrangements for you to stay there."

"Is there anywhere I can buy a razor and a toothbrush?"

"That won't be so easy at this hour, but no doubt we can fix you up."

It was after 10 p.m. when I reached the bed-and-breakfast establishment of Mrs. William Williams. With great kindness my landlady offered to fry eggs and bacon when she learned that I hadn't eaten since lunchtime. I went through to the dining room, where I found my Irish traveling companion finishing up what had evidently been a hearty meal.

"So they sent you too," he remarked. "Now they can keep an eye on us both."

He indicated that I should sit at his table.

"Me name's George Rafferty. Not very Irish, but it's the best I can offer."

"Mine's Thomas Sherwood. How do you do? Did the police persuade you to come here?"

"Persuade, you say! That's good! I was *told* to come here. Young feller, that policeman is going to have something to answer for when he stands in the Judgment Box. Sending an Irishman to Cromwell Road!"

Rafferty seemed to have no wish to leave, for he stayed, talking as I ate.

"And did you lose much in that rucksack of yours?"

"Nothing of real value. A few personal things and a couple of books. The nuisance is that I'll hardly be able to replace the books."

"I cannot conceive that you will not, unless you are an antiquarian, which I hardly imagine is the case?"

I laughed at the implied question.

"No, no, I'm a mathematician, or rather an embryo one. Is there a bookshop in Dublin where I can buy technical mathematical books?"

"That I do not know for sure. But anything you can buy in London you can buy in Dublin, which probably answers your question."

Mr. Rafferty was evidently not as accustomed to hogging 99 per cent of the conversation as Papa Parsonage had been. At the moment his apparent desire to chat was something of a nuisance, for my immediate concern was with Mrs. Williams' handsome plate of bacon and eggs.

"And why would you be wanting to visit Ireland, if it's not impolite of me to ask?"

In view of the hour, place and situation it was somewhat impolite, but I resolved to practice on Mr. Rafferty. Soon I would be telling the same story to the immigration authorities. In many particulars it was substantially correct. I knew that as a liar I was not very convincing, so I had resolved to keep always within a fine margin of the truth.

"Oh, for two reasons, of which frank curiosity is probably the more important. Considering the remarkable changes that are going on in Ireland, this is natural enough I suppose."

"I would say entirely so. Yes, it's great changes that are

25

going on in Ireland. And isn't it a shame to see how backward England is becoming?"

I decided to pass lightly over the last remark. "My grandfather's name was Emmet. We have a tradition that he was a descendent of Robert Emmet's family. I cannot say whether this is really so or not, but certainly I have many relatives in Yorkshire, which I believe is where Robert Emmet came from."

"Ah, that is a fine passport to have in Ireland!" Mr. Rafferty beamed genially. "So you will be wanting to visit the Wicklow Mountains, and the scenes of the last of the Rising?"

"Yes, I'm going to do a little walking in the mountains. But most of my time will be spent in Dublin."

"So it should be," exclaimed Mr. Rafferty with some warmth. "Dublin is the fountainhead of all that is happening in Ireland. Soon it will be the greatest city in the wide world."

Next morning, Mrs. Williams brought the message that I was to call at the police station; my rucksack had been found.

I unpacked it under the watchful eye of Inspector Harwood. Everything was there, including the two books. It bore but one sign of misadventure, a large dark stain across the outside, just where it could not fail to be seen.

"Well, that's certainly satisfactory from your point of view, sir. I wish all the news was as good."

"I am sorry to hear that things are not going well, Inspector."

"I expect you are, for it means more delay, I fear."

"What's the trouble?"

"Well, sir, to be strict I ought not to say, but I expect you'll already have guessed that a body was thrown from the train. We found it in the Severn Tunnel."

"That's certainly very bad—for the body I mean."

Inspector Harwood frowned slightly at this undergraduate sentiment.

"I won't keep you much longer this morning, Mr. Sherwood, but I shall want you to call in here again tomorrow. By then we ought to be in a better position to get to the rights of this matter. In the meantime there is just one further question that I'd like to ask."

"Yes?"

"Can you be perfectly sure that you did not see the ticket collector a second time, the one who opened the lavatory door. When you stopped the train, did he turn up outside your compartment?"

"I can be absolutely certain that he did not. I naturally kept a close lookout for the fellow, but I didn't see him again."

"Thank you. I just wanted to be quite clear on the point."

I lunched on Welsh mussels and brown bread at a café hard by the docks. In the afternoon I discovered a bus that ran into the Gower peninsula. The sea at Oxwich Beach was calm and I had a fine swim, and a fine appetite to boot when I returned to my abode in Cromwell Road. Mr. Rafferty was not to be seen that evening nor next morning at breakfast. Apparently Inspector Harwood had given him his release.

Whether it was the excitement of the last days, or the mussels, or the swim, I awoke sharply during the night with the absolute conviction that someone was prowling about the room. I lay for a moment, immobile with fear, half expecting to be seized by the throat, or to hear the ticket collector breathing sundry gory details in my ear. Then with an enormous effort of will I flung back the bedcovers, rushed to where I thought the light switch must be, fumbled, and found it at last. There was, of course, no one. I tossed fitfully for a good hour before I was able to win my way to sleep again.

In the morning, in friendly sunshine, I found Inspector Harwood with a large pile of photographs.

"Now young man," said he, "I want you to see if you can identify this man Karl or his companion, or the ticket collector, anywhere in this set of faces."

I looked carefully through the pile, but there was no photograph of Karl, or of his companion, or of the ticket collector. But there sure enough was a picture of Mr. George Rafferty. I flicked it onto the table in front of Inspector Harwood.

"This is the only face I have seen before."

"Ah yes, Mr. George Rafferty," remarked Inspector Harwood in a dry voice. "It may interest you to hear that Mr. Rafferty has skipped away; the little Irish bird has flown."

The last of the day was falling as the boat steamed out from Fishguard Harbor. I watched the land receding, the bright land of Wales, until at last it became obscured by advancing night. Perhaps in a few hours I should be back among those green fields, back among those wind-swept uplands, back with the shame of an instant defeat. Worse still, perhaps I should never come back. With these thoughts in mind I turned to the golden glow that still lingered deep in the western sky. Then at last I made my way below to the second-class dining room.

Over a meal of bacon, sausage and tomato, bread and butter, jam and a flagon of tea, I reflected on the four days I had spent in Swansea. Curiously, instead of being annoyed at the delay, I was rather pleased that I had stuck it out, that I had not been tempted to get in touch with Parsonage.

This report would make a far better story if I could recount events on the ship of a similar bizarre quality to those that overwhelmed me during the journey from Cardiff to Swansea. Honesty compels me, however, to say that as far as I am aware there were no singular occurrences during the night. There must certainly have been agents aboard in plenty. No doubt there was a current of intense drama running at a lower level, but it never broke through to the visible surface. In short, I spent an uncomfortable night dozing fitfully in the saloon.

Still more of an anticlimax, I must frankly admit that my passage through Irish immigration turned out to be absurdly easy. It is worth recounting, nevertheless, for my first encounter with the Irish authorities was not without its interest. My interrogator was a large, rubicund man, of just the right type to ensnare an unwary victim, especially after a sleepless night.

"Name?"

"Thomas Sherwood."

"Date of birth?"

"August 29, 1948."

"Occupation?"

"Student."

"Where?"

"Cambridge."

"Father's name and place of origin?"

"Robert Sherwood, Halberton, Devon."

"Object of visit?"

"Curiosity."

"Where do you propose to exercise your curiosity, Mr. Sherwood?"

"Three weeks in Dublin and its environs. One week in the Wicklow Mountains."

"Why are you so curious?"

"No explanation is needed. Everybody is curious about the developments that are taking place in Dublin."

"Why the Wicklow Mountains?"

I told him the story of my grandfather.

"H'm. A Mr. John Emmet, your grandfather?"

He rummaged among a pile of papers, and glanced at one particular sheet. Then, apparently satisfied, "Let me see the contents of your rucksack."

I unpacked slowly and carefully, laying my two books on the table in front of him.

"And how did you come to acquire that great stain across the front of the rucksack?"

I began to tell the story of the lurid events on the train, but I hadn't gone far before he seemed to swell and to become as red as a turkey. Then he broke into peal after peal of laughter.

"No more, Mr. Sherwood, no more. Yes, we know all about what happened on the train. We've got our eyes and ears open, you know."

He wiped a turkey-red face and became more serious as he stamped my passport.

"There. And now away with you. See to it that you keep to your program. You know the rules. Report each week at any guard station. Don't think we like all these restrictions on genuine visitors, but they've been forced on us by the very dubious segment of humanity that has lately been invading our shores. Stick to Dublin and the Wicklow Mountains, Mr. Sherwood, and you'll have a very pleasant holiday."

As I stepped out onto the quayside I could hear his rumbling chuckle. He was of course quite right. No agent in his senses would behave in the way I had behaved. An agent's deepest instinct is to avoid all conspicuous action. None would have squawked as I had squawked.

Next came the short rail journey from Rosslare to Dublin. It was a clear fine morning with promise of a glorious day as I strolled the short stretch of the Liffey to O'Connell Street. Three huge Guinness trucks raced past me. In truth, these people must be heroic drinkers.

I paused for a moment at the bridge, and then walked quickly to College Green. A porter was on duty at Trinity.

"I believe you have a room booked for me. I'm from the other Trinity—Cambridge. Sherwood is the name."

He looked over a list in just the manner that porters have the world over. "Yes, you're in E3, sir. Jim, will you show this gentleman the way to E3?" he called to a passing college servant.

My room contained a wash basin and jug of water. I splashed my face liberally, then stripped and climbed into bed. My last thought, before the mists of sleep overcame me, was to wonder whether Papa Percy had used real blood.

He'd certainly taken no risk of my failing to get into Ireland. Plainly the preposterous comedy on the train had completely deceived Mr. George Rafferty, the little Irish bird—the little Irish agent, more like! But it was depressing that Papa Percy hadn't seen fit to tell me just what was afoot; he evidently took me to be very dumb. Perhaps he was right at that, for until my second interview with Inspector Harwood I hadn't really understood what was going on. The crowning insult was the showing of the picture of poor Mr. Rafferty. Maybe I am dumb, let me admit it, but not quite to that degree.

One last disturbing thought: How was it known that an Irish agent would just happen to be in my compartment? Was every train to Fishguard packed solid with them?

3

————————————————————————————

THE HOUSE IN MARROWBONE LANE

My first day in Dublin passed with little event. I slept until mid-afternoon, had a snack at a rather palatial "self-help" restaurant in Grafton Street, and then spent the hour or two before Hall learning the detailed geography of the college.

I was welcomed at dinner by a live group of students, for the most part medicals and scientists up for the Long Vacation. We went along later to the rooms of one of them, and talked away twenty to the dozen until about 1 A.M.

Apart from this congenially familiar situation, there was a good reason for satisfaction: a product of the suspicious mind with which for good or ill I happen to be possessed. Was it possible that Parsonage had overbid his hand? Had not my passage through immigration been just a little too easy? Suppose the Irish were wise to me, as the Americans say. Would they send me home, jail me or just watch me? Obviously they'd follow me around and see who I contacted. Bad for Mr. Colquhoun! In any case, after the outrageous events on the train, it would manifestly be prudent for them to keep an eye on me, at least for a day or two. Here my association with the Trinity undergraduates would be immensely valuable. No one, not even the most skillful actor, could masquerade successfully as a student in their company. No pretense could possibly survive for more than a minute or two. It would be clear to the authorities that at least in this respect I was exactly what I claimed to be.

At this stage I might add a word or two about my plans, rudimentary as they undoubtedly were. Ostensibly I was to spend roughly a month in Ireland, of which the main portion would be passed in Dublin and its environs. The balance of my visit was to be in the Wicklow Mountains. And I was to report to the police at the end of each week. This then was the official position.

I had decided that I would not break loose from this schedule until the end of a fortnight. I would spend the first week in Dublin. The time would not be wasted, for Dublin was a useful barometer. It is true that the real power of the Irish economy lay to the west, but some measure of it must show itself in the capital city. I would take long walks, checking up on the tremendous building development that seemed to be going on. The speed of this development would give some idea of the strength of the underlying driving force.

After reporting dutifully to the police at the end of the first week, I would go down to the Wicklow Mountains. The whole point of this was to provide a good excuse for my outdoor clothes and mountaineering boots. I would have real need of these over in the west. This was of course the reason behind my Emmet story.

Also it shouldn't be too difficult to find out if I were being followed, once I got into the hills, that is to say. Assuming that I was not, I intended to return to Dublin, check again with the police and then at long last head toward Kerry. In this way I hoped to have a whole week in which to cover my trail before there should be any real foundation for official suspicion, which would of course be roused when I failed to show up at the end of the third week.

The fly in the ointment was Seamus Colquhoun. A visit to Marrowbone Lane was not to be avoided, for I simply did not have anything like an adequate amount of money. But whichever way I tackled this hurdle, there was an awkward stride to be made. Perhaps the best plan would be to put off seeing Colquhoun until the end of the second week. There would then be less chance of my being followed. But would I necessarily find Seamus at home? It would be infuriating to be delayed and to lose part of my solitary week of grace. But if I hied myself to *chez* Colquhoun more or less straightway, I should be maximizing other risks. Suppose Seamus were being watched? The more I thought about the business, the less I liked it. With this reflection I fell at last asleep.

In spite of all I had heard, I was quite unprepared for the tremendous changes that were sweeping through Dublin. The city was being systematically demolished and rebuilt. Whether for some reason of plan or of sentiment, the architectural tidal wave had not yet reached the area of College Green. This was of course why I had not seen it on the first day.

The new layout was of a kind that must surely be unique, for by and large the place was being converted into a vast area of smooth lawns, flower beds and clumps of trees. Dotted here and there were medium-tall buildings, about twenty stories high, some apartments, other offices and shops. The materials were very largely glass and metal, the metal very beautifully colored—bronze, sea blue and delicate yellows shaded like spring flowers.

The geometry of the matter was of course perfectly clear. By the use of tall, but not too tall, buildings, space was being employed far more efficiently than it is in broad, flat cities like London. But instead of using the gain to crowd more and more people into the same area, as Americans have done in all their big towns, Dubliners were wisely laying down floral parks and handsome tree-lined avenues.

All this was surprising enough, but what astonished me more than I cared to admit was the news that it was still less than a year since the whole rebuilding plan was first put into operation. In about ten months almost the whole of the city north of the river had been reconstructed. I resolved to discover something of the methods that were being used, which plainly must be of a novel kind.

This little project proved maddeningly difficult. It was tolerably easy to get into buildings that were nearing completion, and very interesting they proved to be. I spent many hours engrossed in the details of internal layout, lighting, soundproofing of apartments and so forth. But try as I would, I couldn't get anywhere near the early stages of any construction. Every new structure was invariably cordoned off, not just in the immediate vicinity of the building itself, but over an extensive area around it.

It would have been easy of course to break through one of these cordons and to get past the guards. Such irresponsibility was not to be thought of, however. Already I was attracting some degree of attention. A fellow, whom I took to be a detective or security officer, seemed to have a knack of turning up wherever I happened to be. In itself this appeared to be a good sign rather than a bad one. For the man was not at all skillful. He was perhaps just about right for keeping an eye on an inquisitive student, but no counter-espionage service would have employed him on a mission of importance. Even so, I refused to take any unnecessary risk, since it would be absurd to run foul of the authorities over some comparatively trifling incident.

In any case it needed very little to give one the key to the problem. I think it was on the third morning, in the neighborhood of what had once been Winetavern Street, that I caught a glimpse in the distance of a huge mountainous object that seemed to move. At first I thought that my eyes must be at fault, but thinking over the matter afterward I saw the sense of it. I was to see many such moving mountains later on, so I will say no more at present about this particular oddity, except to add that it convinced me of the stupidity of trying to keep the whole business secret. If a casual visitor could ferret the matter out in three or four days, what was the sense of it? The Irish were now making the same silly mistake that the rest of the world had been making for fifty years past. It is notorious how the governments of Britain, the U.S.S.R., the U.S.A. and France have sat on scientific secrets, the same so-called secrets of course, each under the impression that they were unknown to the others. A lot of broody old hens.

One particular building occupied my attention very closely, the new Central Rail Station. By all normal standards this edifice was a sheer impossibility. It was built according to an elegant, bold plan with immensely long horizontal arms of unsupported metal. Even to the most casual eye these arms should have broken instantly under the weight they were required to bear.

I made the best estimates I could of lengths, widths and so on. Then in the evening I looked up the elementary theory of stress and strain—I am ashamed to say I had forgotten it—in Trinity Library. It took an hour or two to clarify my ideas and to seek out the appropriate physical constants—I believe I used the old Smithsonian Tables. But the result was worth the trouble, for the eye had not been deceived. The metal arms in the Central Station were carrying a transverse stress roughly a hundred times greater than they should have done.

More accurately, they were bearing a transverse stress roughly a hundred times greater than a similar piece of metal would have carried anywhere outside Ireland. There seemed but one possible solution to the riddle. I.C.E. must be able to cast metal almost wholly free of the multitude of tiny flaws that greatly weaken the strength of ordinary metals.

I mention this technicality because it greatly fortified my resolve to dig through to the bottom of the I.C.E. business. At about the same time my morale received a fillip in a rather strange way. My rooms were searched.

There was nothing very obvious about it. Probably under normal conditions I wouldn't have noticed the very slight changes in the disposition of my clothes. Over a before-bed cup of tea, I pondered on the situation. Surely it would be incredibly stupid to search my things if I were under any really serious suspicion. All such a search would be likely to achieve would be to put me sharply on my guard. But suppose I was being taken for a slightly overzealous student. Then it might be quite sensible to look me over rather closely, even at the risk of my spotting what was happening. The most sensible conclusion was that Irish Security had some interest in me, but only mildly, at a low level.

Enormously encouraged by these arguments, I resolved there and then to give them a devil of a time. Starting the following morning I tramped assiduously from museum to picture gallery to museum again. Memory is a little dim, but I recollect places in Kildare Street and Merrion Street. Then I thought up a most satisfactory form of torture for anyone who might be deputed to follow me around. I visited the homes and haunts of old Dublin characters. There were the obvious literary men: Shaw, Joyce, Wilde, Le Fanu, Synge.

But I cut a far wider swath than this. My inquiries enfolded such diverse individuals as Sam Lover and the famous Buck Whaley. My high spot was William Conyngham Plunket at No. 18, St. Stephen's Green. This crazy business gave me much quiet satisfaction.

By now the first week was over, and I duly reported without incident to the police. My departure for the mountains to the south was delayed however by the Trinity lads, who press-ganged me into a game of cricket played against a team that fared quite happily under the name of the Dun Laoghaire Wanderers. We won our game with quite a flourish, not let it be said due to my efforts. I had scored a confident 5 when my wicket was totally disintegrated by a beefy individual. The same fellow cracked a tremendous drive at me later in the afternoon, to which I was ill-advised enough to put a hand.

In spite of this inauspicious preparation, the evening turned out exceedingly well. We dined with our opponents, then drank beer and sang such songs as cricketers will. Our team returned by car to Dublin at close on midnight—the match had been "away." The car in which I happened to be traveling stopped at the northern corner of Merrion Square. Two of our chaps got out, and so on impulse did I, assuring the driver that it was no distance at all to Trinity.

I don't know whether it was the beer, or the fluke catch I had held—my hand still seemed red hot—but suddenly it appeared obvious that the time and hour for Marrowbone Lane had arrived at last. When would I be more likely to catch Seamus Colquhoun at home than at midnight on the Sabbath?

The wave of new building had advanced only as far as the area around St. Patrick's. So perforce I had to quit the broad, bright avenues when I reached the old High Street. From now on I walked through the rabbit warren of the Old City.

Very soon, I thought, all this will be gone. Soon Marrowbone Lane will be gone. And what will Seamus Colquhoun do then, poor thing? Soon he and all his kind will be smoked out into the open. Will they run their affairs from an office in one of the bright new buildings? Will they cease selling birdseed or whatever it is they pretend to do at present?

I had already reconnoitered Marrowbone Lane during my tours of the town, so I knew exactly where to find my man, in a little yard set discreetly back from the lane itself. It may be imagined how I made the best reasonable pace I could, first, along Thomas Street, then through the court of the same name, past a block of flats, and so to my destination.

Now what? Here was a slight problem. Should I knock discreetly on the door? I might not be heard, so then I should be obliged to knock discreetly again, and perhaps again, and again. Would this be more likely to attract attention in the lane than one single furious cannonade?

I was silently debating this difficult point when a voice from behind said quietly in a Cork accent, "Not a sound, mister, if you value your life!"

Something was pressed into my kidneys.

"Won't that gun make quite a noise if it goes off?"

"Close yer flamin' beak!" remarked a second voice.

Someone moved in front of me to unlock the door. The gun prodded in my back.

"Quick, inside with you."

"But that's exactly why I came here, because I wanted to go inside!"

Violent hands seized me from the front and heaved me across the threshold, with far more noise than was really necessary. Three of us were crammed into a narrow entrance hall. A door opened and a faint light showed up a staircase immediately to the right.

"What is it, boys?" asked a third voice from above.

"We found a feller on the doorstep."

"Bring him up."

The room into which I was forced seemed somewhat less depressing than might have been expected in the circumstances. Quite incongruously, it was decorated with rather well-done sporting prints. A grandfather clock ticked away in a corner, a fire burned brightly in the grate and a half-filled glass of whiskey stood on a small table.

"Stand over there," said the third voice.

I turned to face them. My captors were both young. The one with the gun was well dressed, almost dapper, like a civil servant; the other, the muscle man who had dragged me inside, looked rather like a character in an Irish play of fifty years ago: cloth cap, heavy rough trousers and shirt without collar. The third man, whom I took to be Colquhoun himself, was middle-aged, dark, bright-eyed, rather full in build, of medium height.

"Mr. Seamus Colquhoun?"

"What's that to you?"

"During winter storms the waves beat heavily on the western strands."

"This is the right moment to buy vegetables on the London market."

"Or fish for that matter, if you have a taste for it."

Colquhoun showed obvious relief.

"You can put it away, Liam," said he, indicating the gun. "This is one of the fellers we've been waiting for."

For the first time since Parsonage gave me the passwords, I really appreciated their effect; no impostor could have chanced on so improbable a sequence.

"You'd best take a look outside, lads."

When the two rough customers had gone down the stairs again, Colquhoun turned on me in a rage.

"What a divil of a time to come here. Are you out of your wits?"

"You didn't expect me?"

"No, nor I didn't anticipate a visit from the Folies-Bergères either. Were you trying to bring the guards down on us? Or have you been at the brewery, drinking the Guinness family into bankruptcy?"

"If you weren't expecting me to come, this is obviously the best possible time; the police won't be expecting you to have visitors either."

"That wouldn't stop you from being seen. You must have been as conspicuous walking the streets as the Nelson Column itself."

"Of course I was conspicuous. I'm not silly enough to slouch about the place. If I'm stopped for any reason, then I'm an innocent who happens to have lost his way. What of it?"

Colquhoun was obviously badly frightened. I realized that he would go on and on unless I took a brusque line. Every minute lost on this rubbish was increasing the danger of the return to Trinity.

"This is a well-nigh perfect illustration of what Shakespeare meant by the term 'unprofitable chat.' I came here to get money from you. I'd like it now, with as little delay as possible."

Colquhoun allowed his anger to settle a little. "How much do you want?"

"Seven hundred."

"That's a powerful lot."

"Which is my business, not yours. Let me have it without any more foolishness, please."

With ill grace Colquhoun left the room. A few minutes later he came back with a bundle of notes. I counted them, and then stowed the roll away carefully in a specially made inner trouser pocket.

"One thing more. I'd like a list of our agents on the Clare and Galway coasts."

"Oh, you would, would you? Isn't that a fine thing to ask?"

"It's a very practical thing to ask, and I'll trouble you for the information. You needn't fear that I'm going to carry a lot of names on a piece of paper around with me, but I want to carry them in my head. I have a pretty good memory, Mr. Colquhoun."

"I'll bet you have, Mr. Sure-sure. Maybe you'd learn a great lesson if I gave you that list. Maybe you'd soon be cooling your heels in jail, or maybe pushing up the green grass of Ireland if you weren't so lucky."

"Is it possible for you to tell me in a simple way what you're driving at?"

There was a glint in Colquhoun's eye as he stared into my face.

"This is the way of it, me fine cock sparrer. There's no list of agents any more, not to mean anything. We've been cleaned out, broken apart. That's what I mean."

"How did it happen?"

"P.S.D." was Colquhoun's cryptic reply. The anger had now subsided. He drank the remaining whiskey at a gulp and slumped down in a chair before the fire. Although I was curious to hear more, it would be wise to move before the fellow launched himself into some new rambling exposition.

"No, you shall not go until you hear the rest of it," he exclaimed when I sought to leave. "Besides, there is something you must do."

"Who or what is P.S.D.?"

"The divil pour me another glass," exclaimed Colquhoun in some surprise. "For a feller who fancies himself as much as you do, you're shockingly ignorant. Or maybe it's a bad joke you're trying to make?"

"Look, Mr. Colquhoun, I'm here on a solitary mission. You are my only contact. When I leave this house I shall have absolutely nothing to do with any of this business you're talking about."

"And that's where you're in for a great surprise, me lad."

"Every minute we spend talking this nonsense increases the risk of my being picked up. So if you have anything really important to say, please stick to the point."

Very deliberately he got up from the chair, fetched an extra glass and poured two overgenerous drinks.

"There's no question of your leaving here tonight. By a miracle you managed to avoid the guards on your way in, but you wouldn't be so lucky the second time."

In this he was probably right. Once morning came and people were in the streets, it would be easier to slip away from Marrowbone Lane. My absence from Trinity would cause no comment either, since I had been intending to leave for the mountains anyway.

"We should have been warned by the experience of the French. They were smashed last year, and P.S.D. were certainly at the back of that. P.S.D. is an organization that started under the cover of a solicitor's business right here in Dublin. Porson, Shilleto and Dobree were the names. Purveyors of Sudden Death, that's what they're known as nowadays."

"Is it some form of Irish counterespionage?"

Colquhoun's laughter was a little hysterical. "Counterespionage eh? It's a great pity the lads aren't around to hear that. Counterespionage!" He sipped his whiskey. "No, me young friend, P.S.D. is espionage pure and clear. The only countering that's done is the counting of profit. What's going on in the west there is worth thousands of millions to the industries of the world."

"You mean that P.S.D. steals and sells trade secrets?"

"That's exactly what I was after telling you, if only you wouldn't always be taking the words out of me mouth."

It crossed my mind that I had yet to meet anyone in Parsonage's outfit who could tell a straight tale.

"The rest of us, British, Americans, Russians, Germans, work maybe a little for the excitement and maybe a little for patriotism, but P.S.D. works only for money. It's business, big business. I can see you're wondering where I come into the picture. Don't make any mistake about me; I'm English, born within the sound of Bow Bell. I've been an operative over here for well-nigh thirty years now."

So this was the explanation of the slight aroma of leprechaun that enveloped all the man's remarks. He was a synthetic Irishman. My determination not to get caught up in Colquhoun's affairs was somewhat weakened by this revelation.

"So I suppose P.S.D. decided to eliminate all potential rivals. How did they go about it?"

"By offering big money to our operatives. When they had pieced together sufficient information against us, all they had to do was turn it over to the guards. They bought out three key men that we thought we could trust."

"How very typical of what happens in all secret organizations. Your so-called friends sell you down the river," I remarked.

Colquhoun looked me over unsympathetically. "See here, mister, sooner or later the Irish are going to close in on this house, maybe tomorrow, or maybe next week, or next month. It'd be easy for me to get to hell out of here, but I don't because I've got a job to do, five jobs in fact. Yours was one of 'em. Where would you have been if you'd found the guards sitting here instead of me? I'll tell you. You'd have been due for a ten-year stretch of hard labor, mister."

He took a smallish notebook from his pocket. "This book has to be got into the hands of the best man left. We're nearly wiped out, but a few pockets are still intact here and there, particluarly to the west. These must be reorganized immediately. Information, names, codes are needed. They must reach the right man without delay."

He tossed the notebook at me. "I can't move meself, and I can't send any of the boys, because the guards are certainly on the lookout for 'em. That leaves you, Mister Cocksure. You are to deliver that little book to Shaun Houseman, who keeps the Unicorn Hotel at Longford. I want it there within twenty-four hours. I can have a car ready for you at ten o'clock tomorrow morning. You say you have a good memory—Houseman, the Unicorn Hotel, Longford."

I put the notebook on the table. "See here, Colquhoun, we'd better understand each other a little more clearly. In the first place I have explicit instructions from London not to get embroiled in your affairs."

"That may be, but this is the gravest possible crisis, and the unwritten law is that we must all do what we can to safeguard the others, just as I stayed here at my post to safeguard you."

There was now very little trace of the Irish in Colquhoun's manner of speech. This was not his real name, I had no doubt. Morally he seemed three times the man he had been before. Whether this was really so, or the effect of a liberal dosing with Power's whiskey, I couldn't say.

"And although I might be able to deliver the notebook, I certainly couldn't guarantee to do so within twenty-four hours. Your idea of a car is ridiculous anyway. I'm here in this country ostensibly as an impoverished student, and I've no business to be found driving a car. If I were stopped by the police I should be under immediate suspicion. And if I were not stopped—well then, you might just as well have sent Liam instead."

I never learned Colquhoun's reply to this argument. We were interrupted by a furious pounding of feet on the stairs. The Irish stage character erupted into the room.

"They've taken Liam," he gasped.

"Where?" demanded Colquhoun.

"Coming down Thomas's."

The only thing to do, and that quickly, was to get into the area of the docks. I grabbed the whiskey bottle and emptied half its contents down the side of my coat. Then I took a small device from my pocket, one that I had made up earlier in the week at the Trinity Chem Lab. It was a long time since I had played with such a thing, not since my school days in fact. I cursed myself for studying mathematics; if I'd done experimental science instead, I'd have felt more confidence in the damned thing working properly. It was bound to be a dud, I thought gloomily as I primed it.

Seamus Colquhoun had drunk too much to be capable of swift action, so I left him to fare the best he could. In a few seconds I was in the street again, trotting as fast as I dared (for the night was dark) in the direction of Cork Street. Soon there was a narrow opening to my right. If I could get through to the docks without meeting a patrol there was still a chance.

I suppose the distance was only about a hundred yards but it seemed much more before a wide space opened up in front of me. There were moving lights to the right and on an impulse I walked toward them, instead of away.

Evidently a posse was searching along the dockside. It would be better to take the initiative by walking right into them, rather than be trapped by a couple of patrols in the streets. Obviously all the approaches to Marrowbone Lane would be blocked.

I lurched forward with unsteady gait, singing but not too raucously.

"Hi there!"

I went on without pause. The challenge was repeated in a louder voice. I stopped uncertainly and glanced around in a vague way. A bright light flashed in my eyes.

"Hey, whashamatter?"

Hands patted my hips and then moved swiftly under my armpits. Who would be fool enough to carry a gun? Liam, I supposed.

"It's all right. The feller's stinking."

Which was perfectly true. The smell of the whiskey was strong, too strong really if they had had the wit to notice.

"Better be on the safe side and take him in. Kevin and Paddy, you go, and get back again as quickly as you can."

We stumbled along to the end of the dock, each man gripping me tightly by an arm. There were three powerful cars.

I was pushed into the back of one and one of the men got in beside me. We had gone maybe a couple of hundred yards in the direction of the castle when I remarked, "Shtop. Want to be sick."

The driver slammed on the brakes—no one likes a vomiting passenger. In a trice he was out and had the door open. His companion forced me onto the pavement.

"Now bring yer insides up, damn you."

I had managed to pull the little package from my pocket, so even though they held me by the arms, I managed to flick it down on the ground as I staggered to the front of the car. Although my eyes were tightly shut the sudden flash almost blinded me. It took but a few seconds to dive into the driving seat, start the engine again and pull away from the dazed guards. I had about five minutes' grace, two or three minutes while Kevin and Paddy recovered their sight, and another couple before they got back to the cars.

I parked in St. Stephen's Green, wiping the steering wheel carefully, and the door handles inside and out, the gear shift, ignition key, and the light switch—there seemed nothing else I had touched with my hands. By now the pursuit would be on, but it would be well-nigh hopeless.

I had only a hundred yards to go when there was the rattle of an automatic rifle. It seemed to come from the west, very likely from the area of Marrowbone Lane. Poor old Colquhoun! Arms were nasty things. Much better to rely on a bit of magnesium flash powder. Lucky the thing had gone off.

There was one more obstacle. I still had to climb into college. One of the lads had shown me the way, and I hated it. First an easy gate, then a stretch along a moderately difficult roof, and lastly a beastly medieval sort of railing with revolving spikes at the top, where the only safe thing to do was to take the whole weight on one's hands. By a kind dispensation I got over it without endangering the next generation of Sherwoods.

To calm my nerve I brewed a pot of tea and consumed a few slices of bread and marmalade. The situation needed close review. I had washed my embarrassingly alcoholic jacket. In an hour or two all excessive traces of whiskey would be gone. It was true that I had been seen, but only in a very poor light. Assuming that the police found no mention of me at Marrowbone Lane, it was highly unlikely that I could be traced. If Colquhoun were taken alive it was doubtful whether he would peach on me, and even if he did it was doubtful whether his information would add up to very much. My impression was that he knew nothing of my mission, nothing of where I was staying, not even my name.

I had the money. I had something else besides. In the moment of crisis I had foolishly snapped up the notebook. Now I was morally committed to visit Shaun Houseman.

4

THE MINSTREL BOY

It was perhaps a little odd that I should have slept well. By the time I had shaved the following morning it was fully eleven o'clock, too late for breakfast in college. So I revisited the cafeteria in Grafton Street, stopping to buy a morning paper on the way. There was small comfort to be gained from the account of the "Death of a Guard," as the *Irish Times* described it:

This paper has had occasion to emphasize only too often in recent months that the ordinary law-abiding citizen of this country is now surrounded by a rising tide of violence. Scarcely a week passes by without some new outbreak manifesting itself, much as an ugly rash may presage the onset of some dangerous disease.

In the early hours of the morning a desperate action took place between the guards and a gang whose headquarters were discovered nearby the docks in the Old City. It is with great regret that we announce the death in this action of Guard Paddy Kilpatrick. Although the desperadoes immediately responsible for his death have themselves paid the ultimate price for this appalling crime, it is understood that one member of the gang managed to escape during the confusion. It is confidently stated, however, that his capture can be at most a matter of hours.

Poor old Colquhoun! Was he really a desperado, or was he a patriot living dangerously for his country, dying fighting for his life? Not for the first time I realized that there are questions with no real answers. I couldn't help wondering how logicians ever came to believe in the principle of the excluded middle. There are so many common examples to refute it.

The bit in the paper about myself was plainly absurd. Such statements are made only if the police do *not* expect to make an arrest; I suppose in the hope of scaring their man into making some false move.

I was more worried by the death of the guard. Had he recovered his sight properly after the magnesium flash? Of course Paddy is a common name, and it might not have been the same fellow.

I intended to travel from Dublin to Longford by a tolerably complicated route. I had no intention of rushing the journey, as I had told Colquhoun in the plainest terms. The wisest plan was to stick to my student pose as long as I reasonably could. My behavior during the past week suggested that I had become greatly interested in the history of Ireland. Very properly this interest could take me to Armagh, where St. Patrick built his cathedral—or, to be less ecclesiastic, where Deirdre of the Sorrows is said to have spent her youth. True, a journey to Armagh would carry me away from Longford, but this was scarcely important compared with quitting Dublin safely, and with gaining some knowledge of travel in the interior of Ireland.

My first experience came as a surprise. I had decided to use buses, since they gave the most frequent and varied transportation, especially in remote districts. I dropped into a bookstore to buy a timetable, only to be asked for my permit. I looked blankly at the girl, "I'm sorry, but do I really need a permit in order to buy a bus timetable?"

"Oh, yes, sir! We should be having all the rag, tag and bobtail coming in to buy timetables if it weren't for the permits."

"Then I must acquire a permit, I suppose. Where can I get one?"

"At any Guard Station, sir."

My first impulse was to go to a Guard Station, but on second thought I decided that the slight risk was not worth the gain. I had no wish to meet Kevin again, remote as the chance of recognition might be.

Besides, I had a better idea. I am ashamed to say that I simply purloined the Trinity Library copy, along with some half a dozen maps of the west. Surely if one needed a permit to buy a timetable, nothing less than special dispensation by the government would suffice for the purchase of a map.

Actually these restrictions were well conceived by the authorities. I found later that there was no hindrance to local traffic. At whatever place one happened to be, information was always available about the local bus service. The genuine resident was therefore put to no inconvenience. It was rag, tag and bobtail like myself who were embarrassed by the restrictions, which I suppose was only right and proper.

After lunch, dressed in cap and tweed jacket, I set off to the bus station, rucksack on back again. I must have seemed a fair approximation of the typical Irish student.

When the bus pulled out of the city into open country I had a severe shock, for the road became truly enormous, a dual carriageway stretching far into the distance, fully a hundred yards wide. It was enormous, judged even by American standards, and it brought home more forcibly to me than anything I had yet seen how great must be the power that was driving this Irish economy.

It struck me that the roads a nation builds provide a fair estimate of that nation's faith in the future. The appalling road system in Britain makes no sense at all, either in terms of economics or convenience, except on the supposition that civilization itself is on the brink of collapse. The bus, too, was huge by any standard I had seen before. It managed the journey to Armagh comfortably within the hour.

I was lucky to get a room in a small hotel. Before starting on my tour of the town I dropped into a café for a pot of tea, it being then about 4 P.M. I mention this detail because a curious incident occurred, one that had a considerable bearing on later events. At a table two places removed there was a group of three: two hard-faced cases, maybe forty years old or thereabouts, and a fresh-faced, pleasant-looking lad whom I took to be about three years younger than myself. The oddity of their association struck the eye immediately. They finished before me. The boy moved first, going over to the pay desk. Really I am exaggerating when I describe the incident as curious. All that happened was a flicker of expression that crossed the faces of the older men, once the younger one had left them together. I couldn't put a name to that expression, but it was an expression that emphatically I did not like. I watched the three climb into a Chevrolet car parked immediately in front of the café.

Alas, there is no sign any more in Armagh of Deirdre, or of the Knights of the Red Branch. Yesterday they proudly walked the earth, alive to the warmth of the summer sun, to the scent of new-mown grass. But they are gone now with all their troubles, gone with their loves and their hates and fears. Soon time's mad, headlong rush will stream past us too, and in our turn we shall be enshrouded in the black obscurity of the past. Soon, you businessmen who walk the pavement beside me, soon you will have wasted the brief flash of life, wasted it in your frenzied concern for pounds, shillings and pence. Soon, you girls, it will be of no concern to anyone whether it is Dick you marry, or Harry, or Tom. Soon, Thomas Sherwood, soon you too will be like a castle in the sand, obliterated by the onrushing tide of life. Soon our whole generation and age will be gone without trace—no, not without trace, for here and there an idea will be preserved and will become a part of the human heritage down the millenniums.

And this of course was the center point of the story of Deirdre herself. It mattered little whether she lived with Naisi or Conchobar. What did matter was the idea that not

48

even the king himself is above his own laws. Was this true of the universe itself?

But this is an intelligence report, not a treatise on philosophy. So I need say no more of my evening in Armagh. I caught an early-morning bus to Cavan. Just outside Monaghan two police cars closed in on us. This was obviously one of the lightning searches that I had heard of, and it gave me the shock of my young life. What a fool to be caught with a bus timetable and a packet of maps! My impulse was to try to jettison the darned things. They were in one of the front pockets of my rucksack, and I thought that maybe I could get rid of them when I lifted the rucksack down from the luggage carrier. Then it crossed my mind that this would be just what the police were looking for. In any case, if they searched me thoroughly, they would find the money.

"Everybody remain seated, please," shouted the conductor. Two guards got into the bus and two stayed outside. Systematically they went through the papers of the passengers. For the most part they passed on quickly, but sometimes questions were asked and luggage had to be brought down from the carrier. It was rather like going through customs. Were the Irish really any better with their present prosperity and restrictions than they used to be in the old days of poverty and freedom? Were restrictions an essential concomitant of prosperity?

My turn was coming up when I had the one great stroke of luck I needed. I suppose that every bus load of passengers must have contained one or two dubious characters. At all events the police found one. In a trice they bundled him out of the bus into one of the waiting cars. When the two guards climbed back to complete their examination, they were already psychologically satisfied men. They had got a case, fulfilled their quota, were ready to be half generous.

I handed over my passport and visa.

"Hey, young feller, your visa is stamped for Wicklow and Dublin. You've no right to be in this part of the country. What's the idea?"

"I wanted to see Armagh. Is there anything very wrong in that?"

"Not if you'd had your visa stamped properly."

49

"But I didn't know that I would want to go to Armagh when I came through immigration. With the best will in the world, you can't always foretell what you will want to be doing three weeks from now."

"You should have checked with the immigration authorities before you left Dublin."

"I can see that now, but I'm afraid it just didn't occur to me at the time."

"And where would you be going on this bus?"

"I'm on my way to Dublin."

"This isn't the way to Dublin at all."

"It is, if you don't have to look at everything with a professionally suspicious mind."

He didn't like this, but I knew it was the sort of remark that a real bad hat simply wouldn't make. I hurried on. "I came up from Dublin yesterday by the direct route, so obviously I don't want to go back the same way. By going via Cavan I can see more of the country."

"How am I to know you left Dublin yesterday?"

"Well, it could easily be checked that I left Trinity yesterday."

"You're at Trinity, are you?"

"Yes, that's my base."

I rummaged in my pocket and produced a bus ticket stub.

"Probably you can verify my statement from this."

He first looked carefully at the stub and then went off for a word with the conductor. When he came back I saw that I had escaped.

"Now look here, Mr. Sherwood, I'm going to give you a chance. It would have served you right if I'd taken you along with that other feller and left you to cool your heels in jail for a couple of days. Remember that as a visitor it's up to you to respect our laws. If you want to go off to any place again, see to it that you check with the proper authorities before you start."

It flashed through me that I must avoid showing any sign of relief.

When the man had gone my neighbor remarked, "Well, he certainly gave you a grilling."

"Yes, it's a bit awkward when you're not used to all these rules and regulations."

This conversation, continuing intermittently right through to Cavan, was a nuisance. Still I managed to make reasonable remarks of some sort and to think over the situation at the same time.

Manifestly I must reorganize my ideas about travel. There must be no more buses, except in emergency. The solution was plain. I must walk, and why not? In a week I could walk across the whole of Ireland. And I must keep well away from these great main roads. I must journey by paths and byways, as bards and tinkers have always traveled from time immemorial. I would not be safe in these tremendous buses, these high-speed modern contraptions, even if I threw away my maps, which was not to be thought of. Besides, I was sure that neither Seamus Colquhoun (God rest his soul, as the Irish would say), nor P.S.D., nor I.C.E. ever traveled in any way except by super-streamlined automobile. Yes, undoubtedly the quiet way was the right way.

But there was one particular bus that I must still catch, the one from Cavan to Dublin. It was more than likely the police would take the trouble to verify that I really left Cavan for Dublin, which I did shortly after 11 A.M., as if I were racing for home like a scalded cat.

The bus stopped to take on passengers in the neighborhood of Stradone. This was what I had been waiting for. I managed to slip away without attracting much attention. It was unlikely that the conductor was in the confidence of the police, but there was no sense in advertising myself by openly asking for the bus to be stopped.

I was now about forty miles from Longford. By nightfall I reckoned on making fifteen miles or more, leaving an easy twenty-five for the following day. I would still be delivering Colquhoun's notebook within three days, just as I had promised. My route lay over the hills to Bellananagh. There I would go quickly across the main road to the south, then to Arvagh, and round the west side of Lough Gowna, along the higher ground into Longford.

As soon as I started along a leafy country lane I knew that my new plan was correct; an indescribable relief from the tension of the past fortnight swept through me. Of course I could not easily have got out of Dublin on foot. I had been right to start with a bus, and I had been lucky to learn my lesson so soon.

I bought provisions in a village along my road and ate lunch in a grassy meadow. I wished I knew the names of the summer flowers. Curious how much better one knows the spring flowers.

By early evening I was well across the main road. My way led along an apparently endless bog road. Mile after mile of open ground lay about me, and I began to wonder where in all this wilderness I could find a place for the night. Not that I had the slightest personal objection to sleeping out of doors, but then one soon acquires an unkempt look. This I wished to avoid, at least until I had fulfilled my commission in Longford.

Sundown was approaching when I reached a small farmstead set in an oasis of pasturage, maybe fifty or sixty acres in area. With the confidence of youth I knocked firmly on the half-opened door. A weather-beaten old farmer appeared.

"I am a traveler, and I wonder if you have a corner where I might lay my head for the night?"

"Will you enter the house?" was the reply, with the courtesy of two thousand years of Celtic culture behind it. "It is a stranger wishing to pass the night," he added to his wife, who was standing back in the shadow so that I didn't see her at first.

"Then he may sleep by the fire. Would he be wanting a morsel to eat?"

I wasn't sure of the correct etiquette here, but since it seemed as if the two had already eaten supper, I answered that I had food in my sack, although a drop of tea would be a great thing to a man who had walked such a long dry way across the bog. This seemed the proper thing, for it soon appeared that neither the farmer nor his wife were anything loath to drink another cup themselves.

I almost choked over my simple meal when in the middle of it the woman switched on a television set. The thing had scarcely been visible before the gloom, nor had I noticed the aerial as I approached the house. It seemed as if two different worlds had come into sharp conflict, and yet why not? This is exactly why television has stopped the drain of population from country to town. Here were two people, apparently isolated in a remote spot, who by the flick of a knob could now find themselves immersed in the maelstrom of human affairs.

How wrong it is to imagine that economics represents the prime moving factor in historical change. Give every man fifty pounds and let him spend it on beer, cigarettes and horse racing, and there will be no historical change to speak of. But give every man a television set costing fifty pounds and there will be a change of significance, a change that may even turn out to be profound. It is not money that is important in itself, but the things that one can buy with money. So much is a mere truism. But it is not a truism to say that what one can buy depends on technology, not on economics. Technology is the key to social change.

I was now getting pretty fit, and I had little difficulty in sleeping through the night in my impromptu bed. The farmer was up by daybreak, which suited me well, for in traveling by foot it is best to reckon time by the sun. I washed and shaved under a pump in the yard, and breakfasted on porridge, bacon and eggs, and of course the inevitable mug of tea. For their kindness the old couple would take little by way of recompense, which was to prove typical of all my experience in Ireland while I was living close to the earth.

Shortly after leaving the farm the pathway turned into a covered lane. At this early hour dew was on the grass and the birds were still singing loudly. When an hour or two later I restocked with provisions in Arvagh, I found to my delight that there was no danger of a repetition of yesterday's experience on the bus. No one seemed to notice as I walked through the sleepy little town. It was of course the situation that the police could not watch every man, woman and child in Ireland, however much they might have liked to do so. With the force at their disposal, all they could do was to watch and raid the places where the chance of discovering nefarious activities was as at its highest. Arvagh was not such a place.

I should like to be able to record that this little pastoral idyll continued through as far as Longford. But it did not. It was shattered by precisely the sort of event that Percy Parsonage had warned me against. The direction of the wind made it difficult to hear the approach of a car. It came furious toward me as I reached the corner of a narrow, twisting road. Barely in time I leaped into the near-side ditch. It was the same Chevrolet I had remarked outside the café in Armagh, and it now contained but two passengers.

With an intense foreboding I increased my pace to a jog trot. About a mile farther on I noticed that a big car had been driven off the road into a fair-sized copse. There were tire marks on the grass, and I followed them for maybe a hundred yards to a spot where a car had been parked. Thick undergrowth had made further progress impossible except on foot, and indeed it was clear from the bushes that were broken and pushed aside, that someone had forced his way through not long before. I pushed along the line of the broken foliage for about five minutes before I came out into an open clearing. There, on ground that no doubt had carried a carpet of bluebells only a month before, was the body of the fresh-faced boy who had kept company with the two thugs in Armagh.

They hadn't even troubled to make sure that he was dead; he had simply been left to die. I gave the poor devil what crude first aid I could, but it was hopeless from the start. I had sat with him for about ten minutes when amazingly he opened his eyes.

"Don't leave me—alone" was the faint whisper.

I gripped his hand tightly. "No, of course I won't, old fellow."

He tried to speak once again, but the best I could catch was the name "Cathleen," and something that sounded like "the cannon with the crown. . . ." Then it was all over.

I closed his eyes and covered him with my sheet sleeping bag. If I had been a real 100 per cent agent, I suppose I would have searched through his pockets, but I had no impulse to do so. I was overwhelmed by a sense of tragedy and could do no more than turn sadly away and retrace my steps to the road.

The immediate problem was how to inform the police. To

make a personal statement to them was obviously out of the question; an anonymous note was better; but best of all this was something I could leave to Shaun Houseman. It was little enough for him to do in return for my delivery of the notebook. I had intended to slip the notebook into an envelope addressed "For the attention of Mr. Shaun Houseman," and simply drop it in at the Unicorn Hotel as I passed by. I had no wish to become embroiled any more deeply in the affairs of British Security, or of P.S.D., or of any of the other Intelligences, or with the sort of goons who had disposed of the young lad. My real business was with I.C.E., and the sooner I got down to it the better I would be pleased.

It was now about 3 P.M. and I was barely twelve miles to the north of Longford. I should be at the Unicorn Hotel comfortably before six o'clock. Three or four miles farther on I was temporarily forced to a halt by a wave of nausea—delayed reaction, I suppose. But the lost time was soon made up, for the nausea was followed by an emotion whose very existence in myself I had never suspected before. I was impelled forward by a wave of cold fury.

The approach into Longford produced a calming influence, however, so that I was able to hunt down the Unicorn with a more balanced mind. A Chevrolet sedan was parked outside. It looked very much like the Chevrolet I had seen three hours before, but, if it was, the number plates had been changed.

I have said already that I am the possessor of a suspicious mind. There seemed now to be no point in declaring my hand, at any rate just for the present. It was obviously a good idea to take a rather close look at the Unicorn Hotel and at its inhabitants, to take a close look at Mr. Shaun Houseman in particular.

I asked for a single room for one night and was told that luckily there had been a cancellation. The register signed, I was shown to a second-floor room by the receptionist. Even while she was showing me the facilities I heard a car start up outside. By the time I reached the window, the Chevrolet was pulling away down the street.

Before dinner I visited the bar. Although it was pretty crowded I saw nobody that I recognized, which in the circumstances was perhaps as well. A man with an air of proprietorship was busy behind the counter. I took this to be Houseman, but I could read nothing from his manner. He looked around fifty, tall, heavily built, putting on weight, hair graying, normal.

I was more fortunate at dinner. I have said that Deirdre and her intimates have vanished without trace. But this I saw must be wrong as soon as I entered the dining room. For she herself was there, alive in all her original loveliness, no longer a queen it is true but a waitress. Surely this must be some descendent of those bygone days. Perhaps the intervening generations had wrought some slight change, for her face was warm and friendly, incapable of the disdain that her ancestor had shown on that last unlucky day.

I was still thirsty from the long walk when she passed.

"Deirdre, could I have a glass of water, please?"

She stopped and stared at me in some surprise, "Me name's not Deirdre, it's Cathleen."

Of course it was, for her face had reminded me of something far less pleasant than the story of Deirdre. This must be the sister of the dead boy in the wood.

5

THE CHASE ACROSS THE COMMON

The position was both delicate and exasperating. Cathleen must be told about the shocking demise of her brother, and that very soon. But when I suggested that we have a word together she took me for a fast stranger with doubtful intentions, which I suppose must have seemed not at all an unusual event. She trotted off in a huff, whether simulated or not I don't know. It took the best part of a couple of hours before I was able to waylay her alone.

I caught her as she came out of the kitchen.

"Look, mister, if you don't go away from me, it's for help I'll be shouting."

Plainly I was not of the stuff that the heroes of American aphrodisiac literature are made, the sort of man the girls chase from cover to cover.

"I want to speak to you about your brother. You have a brother, haven't you?"

This checked her instantly. "What is it?" she whispered.

"We must go where we can talk without being overheard. Come up to my room in about five minutes. It's Number 17." There was no point in having our conversation overheard, and no point in our being seen too obviously together. Metaphorically speaking, I could smell rats all over this hotel.

Announcing herself with a light tap on the door, Cathleen slipped inside. I told her as briefly and quietly as I could all I had seen during the afternoon. She made me repeat my description of the lad's appearance several times, until there could be no doubt that he really was her brother. Then she collapsed in a chair and sobbed quietly and uncontrollably.

I stood around, unable to do anything but offer my handkerchief. Then quickly, so quickly that I was taken by surprise, she jumped up. "Come back, you little fool . . ." I began, but she was gone.

I began to curse silently to myself. In my school days, in the era of scholarships, I used to be afflicted by a recurrent nightmare. I would dream that I was given an examination paper, all the questions of which I could do with considerable facility. Then, just as I started to write out the first of them, there would come an interruption, the invigilator would cry out, "Excuse me a moment, I have an announcement to make. . . ." The announcement would take a quarter of an hour and would be followed immediately by a second interruption and then by a third, and so forth until the whole three hours was over, when once again the booming voice of the invigilator would ring out, "Gentlemen, time is up."

Just as I was handing in my blank paper I would waken, sweating with apprehension.

From the moment I had started on this mission I had suffered one interruption after another. First, Parsonage, who couldn't allow me to get into Ireland in my own way. Then the ill-fated Colquhoun, who hadn't the elementary common sense to see that since his organization had spawned three traitors, there wasn't the slightest reason why it shouldn't spawn four, or five, or six. . . . And now Cathleen, who must whip away on a desperate course without giving me the slightest chance to help her. I had a shrewd idea of what she might be doing, but I couldn't go padding about a strange hotel in the hope that I'd just chance on the right move to make. Better to stay put. A least she'd be able to find me if she wanted me.

I anticipated her return by packing my rucksack. The sooner I could get away from the Unicorn Hotel and from Mr. Houseman the better. Three times I had been asked by the hotel staff for my passport. Each time I had stalled— I hadn't the smallest intention of handing it over. I knew Houseman, with his own background to consider, would never bring in the police, but he must already be aware that I was someone to be watched.

By a miracle Cathleen had managed to find what she wanted. She came in breathing fast, with a file of papers clutched in her arms.

"Let me put them in the rucksack."

She handed them over more trustingly than she should have.

"Come along quickly now. We can creep out by the back way."

Maybe we could and maybe we couldn't. As it turned out, we could. The point of course was that at this hour, 10 P.M., Houseman was heavily engaged in the bar. It would be at least an hour before business became lighter, and maybe it would be another hour or two before he discovered the loss of the papers. Perhaps he wouldn't even find out until morning.

Cathleen had a couple of bikes ready in the lane outside. "Give over the rucksack to me, and you take this," she said, handing me a spade. I noticed that she had a blanket in the

58

carrier on the front of her machine. The next part of our joint enterprise was grimly obvious.

We cycled silently out of the town. I led the way back without difficulty, for it is curious how easily one remembers every detail of a road along which one has walked, in pitiful contrast to the hurrying motorist who sees little and remembers little.

We found the wood again, left our bicycles where the car had been parked, forced our way through the undergrowth. He was still lying exactly as I had left him. I held one of the cycle lamps for Cathleen to lift my sleeping bag. She made no cry, but looked for perhaps half a minute.

"Poor Mickey boy," she whispered, and then added in a small voice choked with passion, "I'll get them for this."

In turn she held the light for me while I dug his grave. Once the spade had cut through the surface turf the ground was rich and soft. I guess it must have taken about an hour before I had excavated a trench about three feet deep. We wrapped him in the blanket and lowered him gently. She wept as I filled in the soil again and replaced the grassy turf.

I put my arm around her shoulders and led her back to the bicycles. We started off along the road, but we hadn't gone far before I saw that the girl was exhausted and on the verge of collapse. Clearly we couldn't ride all through the night. Equally clearly we couldn't go back to the Unicorn Hotel. It would be best to get a few miles away from the wood, and then lay up until morning.

We rode along rather shakily for the first mile or two. I had of course discarded the spade and was able to give Cathleen a bit of a push, but it wasn't at all easy in the blackness. Then surprisingly she began to go along on her own steam, and after a while she took the lead.

"Have you any idea where you're going?"

"I want to go to Morag's cottage" was the reply.

Since I had no idea of the whereabouts of Morag's cottage I had no choice but to follow along. We rode back almost into Longford, but cut away on the east side, crossed the wide main road to Mullingar, and a mile or two farther on started down an unsurfaced lane. There was a solitary cottage rather more than half a mile along.

An old woman answered our knock. When she saw Cathleen she exclaimed, "By the saints, what an hour to be on the road!"

While Cathleen went inside and told the old woman whatever she wished to tell her, I stood outside examining the approaches to the cottage. I put the bikes where we could readily get them onto the road again if we should be in a hurry, for truth to tell I didn't like this cottage business. When he found his papers to be missing, Houseman was certain to begin a frenzied search.

I didn't know of course what sort of an organization he had at his disposal, but it was safest to assume that the organization might be formidable. He would obviously look for Cathleen at every place he could think of, and Morag's cottage might well be one of these. It would have been wiser to have slept in the woods, but Cathleen was so tired that I couldn't find it in my heart to insist. The one comfort was that the lights of a car could be seen approaching the cottage from far off. I thought it most unlikely that anyone would drive that particular night without at least some degree of lighting.

Morag had of course brewed up a pot of tea. She offered me a cup when I came in from the lane.

"And now be off to bed with you," she said to Cathleen.

"Try to get some sleep, but don't take your clothes off," I said. "We might have to make a quick getaway. I'll keep watch, don't worry."

Cathleen nodded, evidently seeing the point.

"Morag, can you tell if a car turns into the lane?" I asked. The old woman answered that she could.

"Then would you be willing to keep a watch, in case I fall asleep?"

"You may be assured that I will."

But I had no intention of sleeping. I took out the file of papers and began to look systematically through them. The first part was scientific, the latter part and the appendices were mathematical. One needed little knowledge of science to appreciate the importance of the first part; it was no less than a description and blueprint of a thermonuclear reactor, the disposition of magnets, currents and voltages, etc. I remembered Parsonage's statement that I.C.E. had produced a working thermonuclear reactor, and a piece of the puzzle became complete in my mind.

Not to make a mystery of the matter I might remark that one of the entries in Colquhoun's notebook read as follows:

Michael O'Rourke (I), sister Cathleen.

The *I* was probably short for I.C.E. Presumably the situation was that Michael had a job at I.C.E. or at least had had the entrée into the I.C.E. territory. It must have been Michael who got hold of the manuscript. In the ordinary course of his business he had brought the manuscript to Shaun Houseman, who must instantly have perceived its fantastic value on the open market. When Michael got wind of Houseman's intentions, he, Michael, had simply been brutally snuffed out. This seemed to make sense, at any rate the sort of sense that one expects to meet in this brand of business.

As I read on, I became more and more uneasy. By now I had reached the mathematical parts. Either my memory was slipping, or there were steps in the various proofs that simply did not seem to follow. At first I thought the stress and strain of the last month, and of the last day in particular, had softened my wits, but bit by bit I found things certainly wrong. I even found an elementary blunder: the statement that apart from an additive constant every monotonic continuous function is equal to the intergral of its derivative. On a grand scale, this was another nonsensical document of the sort that I had already seen in Parsonage's office.

But it gave me some idea of the subtlety of the people I would soon be dealing with. Evidently I.C.E. had a deliberate policy of turning out spoof documents, which they fed to the foreign agents much as one might fling hunks of poisoned meat to a pack of snarling wolves. Poor Michael! This was something that I must be careful to keep from Cathleen.

I must have dozed off round about dawn, for I was roughly wakened by Morag.

"Away with you. They're coming up the boreen."

The lane was a little more than half a mile long. Assuming

the car came quickly along the very rough surface, it would take the best part of a minute, sixty precious seconds, of which Morag must have consumed ten. I took five more to get upstairs to Cathleen's bedroom, another five to drag her out of bed, ten to get her downstairs and a final ten to grab my rucksack and the file of papers and to race out after her to the bikes. This left twenty seconds to reach the turn of the lane beyond the cottage before the car appeared. We managed it with nothing to spare.

The car would stop at the cottage, but not for long. However skillfully Morag prevaricated, we had left obvious signs of our flight. It occurred to me that I ought to have left the papers behind too. This would have delayed them longer and might even have caused them to call off the pursuit altogether.

We came out of a thin wood into open fields, and my heart fell, for there were gates across the path. I fretted at the precious seconds that were lost in opening the first of them— the car had started again. But it was the gates that saved us. It takes longer to open a gate from a car than from a bicycle, and what we gained in this way made up for the extra speed of the car on the stretches between.

It must have looked a preposterous race to an onlooker. I would forge ahead, slide off onto one of the pedals, jump down and half open the gate. Cathleen following behind would ride through and head for the next gate at full speed. Meanwhile I would slam the gate, making sure it was firmly shut. By the time I reached the next one, Cathleen would have it open and I would ride through and then head for the third and so on. By this technique we kept the car at bay, a couple of fields behind, and certainly out of shooting range.

At length we came to what I had been hoping for, a stout gate that simply couldn't be opened. I lifted the cycles over. This cost some time— I could now see Houseman in the front seat by the driver. But the great thing was that they could not lift the car over, and to attempt to batter a way through would be to risk damage and delay.

Looking back I saw that we had won. The big car was being slowly turned. Another couple of hundred yards along

I saw why. The path—it was now no more than a farm track —ran between stone walls which narrowed here and there enough to prevent the transit of any but the smallest vehicle.

We came out onto what in England would have been described as a common. I knew it stretched away to the southeast as far as the huge trunk road from Cavan to Athlone. My plan was to ride as far as we could in this direction, but more of this later.

The immediate danger was that Houseman would get his car onto the common by some other route. We therefore pushed ahead as hard as we could go. After a mile or two, patches of bog appeared. This was good, because it would make the use of a car extremely hazardous. And indeed there was no sign of any car, presumably because Houseman knew the difficulties—it really takes very little in the way of an obstacle to turn this particular form of transportation into a mockery, just a very short stretch of soft ground. Twice we had to lift the bicycles over belts of bog and peat hags that I thought would be sufficient to stop even a jeep.

I learned from Cathleen that there was ample cover within a mile of the main road—trees and bushes, in contrast to the open ground we were now crossing. This seemed to solve the whole problem. It would be useless for Houseman to try to intercept us at the road. All we had to do was to lie in cover until a bus was due— I had my precious timetable. At the right moment we would simply mount onto the road, flag the bus to a standstill and then away! (This was an occasion when the risk of public transportation must be taken.) Everything was easy. I discounted an attempt to follow us on bicycles; they were much too far behind for that. Horseback might be a good idea, but I doubted if horses would be ready saddled.

And on this basis I allowed the pace to slacken, not to a dawdle by any means, but to a pace more congenial to a tired girl. In this I grievously underestimated my opponent. I want to emphasize this point because a great deal followed from my mistake. Just as two streams, a couple of hundred yards apart, on opposite sides of a watershed, separate implacably to their respective oceans, so this was the point of divergence of my story. If I had hurried Cathleen along I think I would have married her. I think in the long run I would have taken a comparatively lucrative job with I.C.E. (knowing the situation as I do now), and I think we would have settled down to raise a family in peace and quiet on the coast of Kerry. But because I allowed her a breathing space, scenes of horror were to follow in the short run, and in the long run I was to solve the secret of I.C.E.

I was extraordinarily slow in spotting the form of Houseman's attack. At first I thought that some enterprising farmer must be early at work. We had ridden for maybe ten minutes before I realized that the noise was too loud for just one tractor. Surely every farmer in the district couldn't have employment for such an implement at six o'clock in the morning?

Not until we mounted a low hill could I convey a real sense of urgency to Cathleen. Some two miles back, perhaps a little more, four caterpillar tractors were heading in our direction.

Even now I was not seriously alarmed, for at our accelerated pace I thought we must be moving quite as fast as the tractors. We couldn't be much more than six miles from the road, and after five of these we would be in cover.

But I was not reckoning on a sudden change of the ground. Quite suddenly it altered from the smoothness of the common to coarse, tussocky grass. We began to bounce and to lose speed. The tractors would hardly be affected. The position was plainly desperate.

There was nothing for it but to abandon the bikes. We could make better time now on foot. At this stage we were about three miles from the cover by the road; the tractors were two miles farther back still, five miles from cover. On this rough terrain they would probably take half an hour to do the five miles. Could we run three miles in the half hour? Without my rucksack, and alone, I believe I could have done it. But Cathleen was no faster than I could manage with the rucksack, so there was no point in discarding it.

I will not dwell unduly on the painful slowness of the following minutes. Nor was it only time that seemed to go "on leaden feet." We ran until I thought that my lungs would burst, and yet at every stride the tractors closed the precious distance.

Next there came a long stretch of rough uphill ground which had to be taken in the face of quite a fresh breeze. Everything depended on the other side of the hill. With a great effort we would reach the top two or three hundred yards in the lead. If there was reasonable cover on the other side we should be safe.

With every muscle screaming for rest we arrived at the top. Ahead was the best part of a mile of open ground, and then, only then, a plethora of trees and bushes. The tractors would run us down before we could cover half this distance.

If only we had hurried back there on the common. If only we had gained ten minutes. If only—but this was the lesson of life compressed into a single hour.

Then I had an idea. I shouted to Cathleen to run on. With fumbling fingers I tore open the rucksack and pulled out the papers. I could see the drivers clearly by now, grim-faced men in cloth caps. Houseman was a passenger in one of the machines, a great fat slug clinging to the rolling monster. But this would give him a problem to think about. In a gust of wind I released the pages of the manuscript. As if to show its contempt for this appalling rubbish, this desecration of Lesbesgue, the breeze lifted the sheets. Within a minute they were scattered over a couple of acres or more. If they were to be retrieved, Houseman would have to act instantly, for even on the ground the sheets chased along at a merry pace in the direction from which we had come.

There was never any question as to what would happen. Houseman jumped down to retrieve one of the pages, took a quick look at it, and began shouting order at his band of hoodlums. Even at the risk, I paused to watch them. The scene became ludicrous beyond my fondest hopes. In a sort of fantastic polo game the tractors wheeled hither and thither. Every so often a man would leap down from his seat, and another piece of nonsense was gathered to the fold. Chuckling mightily, I trotted after Cathleen, a modern Milanion anxious to claim my Atalanta.

I saw already that something was wrong, even when I was fifty yards from Cathleen. Her eyes blazed with furious anger.

"You——," she flared.

I suppress the word not because it was a particularly bad one—I had heard worse often enough before—but because this was the only time I ever heard her make such a remark.

"And me poor brother not dead in his grave these twelve hours," she added.

Now I saw the appalling thing I had done. I had casually tossed away the manuscript that Michael gave his life for. I had thrown it to his murderers, and I had done so with a laugh. I started to explain, but then I saw the hopelessness of the real explanation. It's perfectly true that in the best society one does not integrate the derivative of a function. But can one expect such a remark to appeal to a pretty girl in an extremis of anger? Of a surety one cannot.

So I tried an appeal to common sense.

"Look, Cathleen, if I hadn't scattered your brother's manuscript to the winds we'd have been caught by the tractors. And if we'd been caught, Houseman would have got the manuscript anyway. In fact he'll find it harder to get the papers out from the bog than if he'd only had to take them from my rucksack."

This cold logic calmed her a little. But she hammered a fist into the palm of her hand. "At least you should have fought for it."

No remark could have been better calculated to destroy me. Once again I spluttered with laughter. The trouble went back to my nursery days. I had puzzled for the best part of a couple of years over a little piece that went something as follows:

> A asked for it.
> B bit it.
> C cut it.
> D dug for it.

I remember that F fought for it, S sought for it, M mourned for it and that T, most sensibly, simply took it. The problem that worried my childish mind was the nature of "it."

"Oh, well, if that's what you're thinking of me, I'll be going my way," said Cathleen.

The humor was gone.

"That you will not. There's still danger from the road." Which was perfectly true. It was by no means impossible that Houseman had sent a carload of thugs round by the road with the idea of heading us off. If so they were too late, so long as we didn't stand around arguing futile nonsense. I seized Cathleen by the arm.

"Come on, girl, you can say all you want to say once we're safely away from here."

It would make a nice ending to this episode if I could claim a final encounter with the Houseman gang, there among the trees and bushes. But a hundred men might have searched all day in that wonderful cover and never had sight or sound of us. We reached the road and lay down to wait for the next bus toward Athlone. I judged from my timetable that one would go by somewhere between 8:20 and 8:30 A.M. We had only half an hour to pass.

It seemed that the best place would be to leave the bus near a small place called Tang. Cathleen was of a different mind.

"It's to Athlone I'm going."

"But that's exactly where Houseman will be looking for you, if he wants to look for you."

"Maybe it's me that'll be looking for him."

I passed this by. "The towns are a bad idea, Cathleen. I doubt if I could stand up even to a routine police inspection."

"Then it is right for you to stop at Tang, and I will go to Athlone."

"But it's only sensible that we should stick together."

"After what happened back there on the bog, do not think that I will go with you."

A vision came to me of the pages of manuscript fluttering in the breeze, Michael's life blood.

"Tell me what better I could have done?"

She refused to meet my eyes. "When I go with a man, it will be with a man who knows how to behave in trouble."

I heard a fast-moving heavy vehicle away in the distance, which was perhaps as well, because I don't think I could have found an answer to this last remark.

"Stay here until you see that I've managed to stop the

bus." I climbed down a bank and upon the road. There was no point in exposing us both to the risk of a chance shot.

I booked two single tickets, one to Athlone and one to Tang. As the bus raced along, I made one last attempt to persuade Cathleen not to continue to Athlone. The fleeting moments soon passed. We drew up to my destination, and I remembered to give Cathleen a note, for she was without money.

"But how will I repay you?"

"Don't bother, it's little enough," and I added unkindly as I pulled my inevitable rucksack down from the carrier: "When you meet up with someone who behaves well in time of trouble, give it to him with my compliments."

I dropped off the bus and turned into a country road. So it came about that Cathleen and I parted for the first time.

6

THE JOURNEY TO THE SOUTH

The hardest decision of my life was to leave the bus at Tang. The temptation to head a campaign against Houseman seemed almost irresistible. Cathleen would have joined me because of her consuming desire to avenge Michael's death. I had Colquhoun's notebook. With its help it might have been possible to organize some reliable nucleus, after which I didn't think the outwitting of Houseman would have been an excessively awkward job.

It is difficult to analyze the reasons why I didn't do so. Certainly they had no connection at all with Parsonage's warnings and wishes. His organization creaked and groaned so badly that my awe of him, if it ever existed at all, had blown away with the west wind. At the time I believed it was I.C.E. that swayed the balance. I was beginning to realize that I.C.E. must simply be toying with its opponents, and must be having a good laugh at them in the bargain. So it seemed quite futile to build up an organization that in its very nature was defeated from the start. Why not attack the problem right at its source? This, I say, was the reason I gave to myself. Looking back, I realize now that pique may have had something to do with it.

My plan was very simple, which seemed a good recommendation at the time. But I was soon to learn that it is possible to be too simple, both in plan and in mind. My route lay pretty well along two sides of a right-angled triangle, first a walk of about 120 miles to the south beyond Tipperary, then a drive to the west along much higher ground. There would be no stopping at farms and cottages during this last push, which would carry through from the region between Mallow and Cork, over the highest mountains of Ireland, right into the central peninsula of Kerry. I aimed to make the last eighty miles in two or three forced marches, if necessary during night hours.

One of my first acts, a rite, was to burn the notebook. I had a fair portion of it stored away in my head, so there seemed to be no point in continuing to carry around such a dangerous document. Perhaps I should have handed it to Cathleen, but I thought probably not. As I watched the pages turn to ashes, I felt that at long last I was freed from my embarrassing connections. Once again, an error.

During the week that followed, I had a greater ease of mind than at any later time, right up to the end of the whole business. I moved with the sun, lying out in grassy meadows reading my books, sheltering from the rain. I slept well at night on hard beds, and sometimes on the harder ground. This was a gentle country I was walking in, without any suggestion of the wider horizons of moor and mountain, of sea and storm that lay no great distance away on my right hand.

As I tramped along I would sometimes think over what I

had learned of I.C.E. Of the technological achievements of this organization I had now built quite a catalogue. It ran like this:

ITEM. Masters of metallurgy. To wit the horizontal metal girders of the Dublin Rail Station.

ITEM. Builders of tremendous earth-moving equipment used to construct enormous roads among other things. Example, the "moving mountains" I had seen in Dublin. Probably powered by nuclear engines.

ITEM. Producing a very large electrical output. In addition to own uses, was now supplying power to even the most remote country cottages. Power must come from nuclear origin since no appreciable imports into Ireland of coal and oil. Possibly derived from water by thermonuclear process.

ITEM. Vast output of fertilizer. Much of the farmland around me had been reclaimed from bog.

All this added up not just to a great industrial organization, but to a new world, a new civilization. It may sound a little odd but I was even more impressed by the things that I.C.E. was not doing. They were not making cars—or tractors for that matter. All these were imported from abroad. Why? I believed I knew the answer. Because these were products that could adequately be manufactured elsewhere. I.C.E. was so incredibly confident in itself that it was only doing what others could not do. It scorned to engage in any well-understood industrial process.

But of *how* all this was being done I hadn't learned enough to spread on a farthing. I knew of course that many clever scientists had joined I.C.E. I knew the names of a fair number of them. But clever as they were, there were men just as clever outside Ireland, at my own university for instance. So this could scarcely be the whole answer. I thought over every possibility that even the most rigorous racking of brains could produce, but nothing that came to mind seemed remotely plausible.

I passed Tipperary on its western side with the intention of skirting the Galty Mountains. My idea was to keep to the south until I reached a point a little beyond Fermoy, and then at last to swing sharply to the west. By taking this route (which was not the nearest) I would avoid getting close to I.C.E. territory at too early a moment. It was likely that the border would be protected in depth. This being so I wanted to tackle it as a Rugby player makes straight for a touchdown. I had no wish to be flanked out to the wings.

As I say, I was to the west of Tipperary, I suppose near on ten miles. It was now coming up to six in the evening, so I set about finding a resting place for the night. I discovered a farm under the slopes of Slievenaman. It was rather larger than I would have wished, but there seemed to be no reasonable choice. My request for a bed was met with a refusal. "It is unlucky for you that we have visitors already," explained the woman of the house.

"There is no problem in that," remarked a rich voice behind me. I turned to find a clergyman smiling at us.

"There is no reason why he shouldn't share the loft with Tiny."

"That would be very fine if your Reverence has no objection."

"I am only too glad to be of help to a passing traveler. Mrs. O'Reilly will get her young lad to show you the way. After you have washed, perhaps you would care to eat supper with me."

I thanked him warmly and departed for the loft, following behind Mrs. O'Reilly's lad. There were two beds, and Tiny was sitting on one of them. He was a gigantic fellow, the sort who plays center position in American football, fully 250 pounds. He responded to my look of astonishment with a lazy smile, a cigarette between his lips.

There was a pot bowl and an urn with water, so I stripped to the waist and began washing. During this operation, while I was soaping my face and my eyes were shut, a vise seemed to close on the biceps of each of my arms. I struggled violently to free myself but without the slightest success. Suddenly I was released. I opened my eyes, but soap got in them, smarting furiously. Somehow I got hold of my towel.

"You bloody great ape," I yelled. For it was Tiny. He had sneaked up absolutely silently behind me and had gripped me with his huge hands. Now he burst into bellows of laughter.

I did the best I could to seem unconcerned. I finished washing, put on a clean shirt and wished heartily that I had never come near the place— I had not taste for spending the night with a gorilla, one that apparently possessed the sense of humor of an eight-year-old child. I considered whether or not I should pack up and leave there and then, but decided that to do so would be abominably discourteous to my clerical friend. I had better stick it out.

At supper the cleric seemed to detect some reserve in my manner. "Has Tiny been upsetting you?" he asked.

"No, no, nothing of any importance."

"He is apt to be a bit playful. But I'll have a word with him. You will have no further worry I can assure you. He's really a very good fellow, you know, extremely faithful."

"Do you spend much time in these parts, sir?" I said, thinking it best to change the subject.

"Often, when I am free from my charge in the city of Cork. But from your speech I would say that you yourself are from England, from the west?"

"Yes. I'm a Devon man by origin. I'm enjoying a few weeks' rambling here after finishing my finals at Cambridge."

"Aha, from Cambridge, a great place I've heard. You are a fortunate young fellow. By a sad dispensation we have far too few visitors from abroad nowadays."

"Can you explain why that should be, sir?" said I, steering the conversation away from myself and my affairs.

"There is no mystery about it, I fear. The mammon of unrighteousness is upon us."

This sort of remark I can make no sense of, so I left the man to extricate himself, which he did without difficulty.

"Aye, it is a great sin that hangs on us, better it were a millstone."

"I cannot say that I've seen very much to support your point of view, sir."

"Believe me, Mr. Sherwood, the young look only to outward symbols. They do not see the maggot busily at work rotting the core of our national life."

"I take it, sir, that you are referring to I.C.E."

"I am indeed," he boomed. "The monstrous iniquity that is fast robbing us of our ancient way of life."

"The ending of poverty is all I have seen on my travels."

"Man does not live by bread alone. That is as true today as it ever was. With increasing prosperity the old virtues, the old sense of values, are all fast being lost, irretrievably lost."

"Do you think prosperity and virtues are mutual enemies then?"

"Remember the words of Our Lord, Mr. Sherwood, 'It were easier for a camel to pass through the eye of a needle . . .' Better to be poor, and sound in moral wind and limb, than to live in the finest earthly mansion."

"I simply can't agree that poverty is a desirable end in itself, sir. Poverty may often seem virtuous just because it's given no opportunity to be anything else. I'd rather say that only in wealth and prosperity can true morality be judged."

He laughed with a rich chuckle. "How delightfully argumentative you modern people can be!"

"I take it that there is a very general agreement in the Church on this subjct of I.C.E.?"

"One good thing, and one good thing only, has come from the growth of the hosts of the ungodly: my Church and the Church of Rome now stand nearer together than I would have thought possible."

This explained something that had puzzled me. His dress had seemed different from that of the priests I had seen in Dublin. It was of course the dress of the Church of Ireland. Both my powers of reason and observation were being dulled by so much country air.

I will not attempt to describe the rest of what (to be frank) I found a somewhat tedious conversation. I was a little surprised to find myself rallying staunchly to the defense of I.C.E. but I had yet to see anything of this organization that offended my sense of morality—such as it is.

The time came when I could decently suggest retiring for the night. I had no particular wish to renew the unpromising acquaintance of the gorilla, but this had to be done sooner or later. It was a relief that my clerical friend had not forgotten his promise to speak a word of caution to "Tiny." He came across to the loft with me, took the gorilla aside for a few moments while I made up my bed and then remarked, "I think that all will now be well, Mr. Sherwood. What time would you care to breakfast in the morning?"

"Would seven-thirty be too early?"

"By no means. What is the time now, I wonder?" He pulled out a watch attached to a chain. It was of the kind that one must snap open before the dial can be seen.

"Ah, nine-thirty. Early to bed, eh, Mr. Sherwood?"

I was hard put to it to make any suitable reply, for on the inner cover of the watch I caught a glimpse of a most disturbing design. Stamped in the metal was the imprint of a crown.

I knew now the meaning, or at any rate a part of the meaning, of the words of the dying Michael—the cannon with the crown. I had had the word "cannon" all wrong. It should of course have been "The canon with the crown."

My strong impulse, once the canon had gone, was to pack my things and to be away with all haste. Whether I had betrayed my surprise at the sight of the watch I cannot say—I may well have done so. At all events I couldn't avoid the suspicion that the gorilla had been detailed to watch me closely. He stood by the door, a cigarette on his lips, smiling his lazy smile. Regretfully I decided it would be wiser to stay than to try to go.

I lay in bed thinking distasteful thoughts and keeping a wary eye on the gorilla. My after-dinner conversation with the canon just didn't ring true. All those phrases, "mammon of unrighteousness," "earthly mansions," are the sort of thing a cleric will say from the pulpit, but not any more in ordinary social talk. The man was an impostor, grossly so.

The night was at best unpleasant and at worst terrifying. Eventually the gorilla decided to turn in—his bed came between mine and the door, I noticed. The light went out. I lay listening to his breathing, to make sure that he didn't get out of bed. Nothing happened for maybe an hour. Then very stealthily he did get out. I heard him prowling almost silently about the room, and I had the horrible certainty that he was going to seize me again. It needs not the slightest imagination to realize the impelling desire I had to reach the door or the lights at least, but I knew as if by divine revelation that the one thing I must never do in front of this creature was to show fear. He came quite close, and then of a sudden let out in the dark his ear-splitting bellow of laughter. Drawing on every particle of my will power I roared back, "Get back to your bed. If I have any more trouble I'll go straight and fetch your master."

He went back. I decided that since he hadn't attacked me the safest thing would be to seem unconcerned, really to try to sleep. I think that I managed to do so in a nightmarish fashion.

When morning came at last I was up betimes. I noticed that no sooner did I jump out of bed than the gorilla did too. I shaved, washed and packed my rucksack, all quite deliberately. Then I went down into the farmyard. Although it was still only seven o'clock, I eventually decided to go into the house and to wait there for breakfast. By so doing I hoped to escape from the ever-watchful eye of the gorilla.

In my story thus far there have been occasions when luck has rather decisively taken my side. Indeed I realized once or twice that I had rather been overdrawing my account in this respect. Now, in an instant, I was called on to repay my borrowings, at a usurer's rate of interest. The canon was already abroad. He was seated at the dining table. When I came in he looked up with a placid smile. By his side was Shaun Houseman. Then I saw the enormity of what I had done. I had walked unawares into the headquarters of P.S.D.

I remember once playing in a game of cricket in which my side was called on to face up to a couple of quite ferociously skillful bowlers. Before we started our innings one member of the team marched around the pavilion advising us all that the one hope was "to take up a hostile attitude." We duly took up a hostile attitude and were dismissed for a total of less than thirty.

In a rather similar way I now felt that my one hope was to seize the initiative. "Well, well, Mr. Houseman! And did you manage to recover all those papers from the bog?"

Houseman scowled at this mock-cheerful greeting, but the canon looked carefully at his manicured nails and said, "As a matter of fact one or two pages *are* missing, Mr. Sherwood.

I am hoping for your own sake that you will be able to tell me what was in those pages."

"What particular piece of nonsense have you in mind?"

The canon was still looking at his hands. "I would advise you to explain very clearly what you mean by that remark, Mr. Sherwood, or you may find that I am a less patient man than I seem."

"There isn't the least uncertainty about my remark," I said with a bold show of confidence. "The manuscript was an obvious tissue of rubbish from beginning to end."

I suppose he stood to lose several millions on the matter, so it was scarcely surprising that this last statement brought the examination of his fingernails to an abrupt end.

"Houseman, get me the case."

Houseman fetched a brief case to the table and took out a file, which he handed to the canon.

"Now show me exactly what you mean."

I opened up the file. These were the papers all right, considerably stained from their wind-swept flight across the bog. I started reading quite slowly from the beginning.

"I am not prepared to sit waiting for very long, Mr. Sherwood. If I lose my patience with you I shall call for Tiny," announced the canon. This was the psychological crisis. I had but a single card in my hand, my technical competence. I must seek to get this one card rated at its highest possible value.

"Look, sir, I've already given you a quick assessment of this document. Now I'm going to give you a detailed assessment. But you'll have to wait my time for it, not your own."

He gave in, as of course he had to, if he wanted to get any decent information. Once he had the information, it would be soon enough to send for Tiny.

I set to work neither too hastily nor too slowly. Breakfast was brought for Houseman and the canon.

"I'll have mine too, Mrs. O'Reilly," I said, without looking up. My breakfast was brought. By playing my one good card at least I had won the first round. But would I win any more than the first?

Someone brought in my rucksack. The canon went through the contents. He was interested in the books, which he examined rather closely. I have the habit of annotating my books with marginal comments.

When at length I had finished, I pushed the file across the table. "Well, there it is. I won't guarantee that I've found all the mistakes, but you can see for yourself that the ones I have found show up the whole thing for a piece of complete nonsense."

Instead of attempting to understand anything of what I had written, the canon simply compared my handwriting with the annotations. The two being the same, the evidence against Houseman's document must now have looked very strong, particularly since spoof documents were presumably fairly common anyway.

Something else in the rucksack interested the canon: my only weapon—a packet of magnesium flash powder. He opened it up, lit a match and set the stuff off in one big puff.

"Very pretty indeed. By the use of some such material a person unknown (as the police say) made quite an ingenious escape from the Dublin guards a week or two ago. On the sixteenth of July, if I remember correctly. Where would you have been on that day, Mr. Sherwood?"

"In Dublin, as a matter of fact."

"A strange coincidence, I must say! And now would you be so good as to tell me why you happen to be in Ireland at all."

"Oh, there's no mystery about that. Our people in London are very worried by the high percentage of dud stuff that's been coming through. I was simply sent over to help separate the wheat from the tares."

He was now very calm again, his voice purring like a huge cat. "Our meeting is indeed a fortunate one from your point of view, Mr. Sherwood, for I fear you would have found little employment for your talents if a kindly providence had not brought you to my door yesterday evening."

"I was beginning to realize that, sir. I'd be glad to hear what terms you have to offer!"

He laughed in a melodious, insincere fashion. "My dear young fellow, need I remind you that a guard was killed during that little operation of yours last month? And you ask me for terms—terms!"

"I cannot imagine there was anything very unusual in that, nor can I imagine that the rest of your men are content to work for nothing."

"What a very mercenary young man it is. Ah well, we shall see what we shall see. Quite a number of documents need to be looked over. When they are finished and I have studied your reports, then perhaps we can reopen this conversation."

Houseman had said nothing throughout this interchange. From his sour expression I could see he had no liking for me as an ally. He started to protest, but the canon silenced him with a gesture.

Many features of the situation were far from being reassuring. But at least the scoundrels had some need of me. And I had a promising idea stirring in the back of my mind. Even so, I was not prepared for the cunning of the canon.

After breakfast they bundled me into a car, not a Chevrolet. Houseman drove, with the canon beside him. I sat in the back with Tiny. No attempt was made to conceal the route from me. Near Galbally we turned off on a mountain road, unpaved and of a width not much greater than the car itself. The road wound upward in an easterly direction, the higher slopes of Galtymore lying two miles or so to the south.

We had climbed perhaps a thousand feet by the time we reached our destination, which I had better describe in a little detail. There was a cluster of buildings, the main one a rough-hewn, single-story stone cottage, well built to resist the challenge of any storm. I soon discovered it to have three small, boxlike bedrooms, together with two rooms each about fifteen feet square. One served as a parlor, the other as a kitchen. The parlor faced to the north, away from the high mountain. One could look down a long stretch of bog toward the head streams of the river Aherlow. At the present season of the year this northern aspect was tolerable, but in winter it must have been an appallingly gloomy spot.

There were two main outbuildings, one a garage, the other a square concrete affair with a small high window—the only guess I could make as to its function was most unpleasant to say the least. It was a guess that subsequently turned out to be correct. The conveniences of the establishment were situated to one side of the garage, about thirty yards from the cottage.

The canon led the way into the cottage and to the sitting room. Houseman followed, carrying two large brief cases, which he proceeded to unpack. A very considerable pile of papers was disgorged. The canon indicated them with a gesture.

"This you will agree, Mr. Sherwood, is a place where you can have absolute quiet, where you will be free from all unpleasant disturbances. Tiny will see that everything is in order and will prepare your meals."

"We still have not settled the terms of my employment, sir. This is an awful lot of work to undertake."

"No doubt, Mr. Sherwood, no doubt. And yet I think you will readily undertake it, for you see I am accustomed to getting a little annoyed with clever young men. Tiny is quite extraordinary in his devotion to me, Mr. Sherwood. As you might guess, he simply detests people who give me cause for worry."

"I think you are going the wrong way about it, sir. Good scientific and mathematical work cannot be done under duress."

"An interesting proposition, but one that I have no doubt is quite false. I shall return here in about two weeks, at which time I shall expect to find that you have completed a set of coherent, accurate reports on the whole of this material."

Not to be done out of the last word, I remarked that I would do the best I could, but that it was asking a great deal. Throughout this conversation Houseman had fidgeted about in an uncomfortable way. Quite evidently he was worried by the canon's glib smoothness. Equally evident, if Houseman had cause to be worried I had a double cause for anxiety.

Indeed I was beginning to feel that Tiny was to be preferred to the canon, which was just as well, for shortly after midday Houseman and the canon drove away. I was now left in a remote desolate spot, a wilderness of bog to the west, north and east, a wilderness of rock and mountain to the south; alone with a monster strong enough to cripple me with the utmost ease should he feel so disposed.

7

THE END OF P.S.D.

The idea that had occurred to me back at the farmhouse was probably a good one: to play along with the canon and his band of zanies until they acquired confidence in me. Then it would be natural for them to send me into I.C.E. territory, for I could ostensibly be of far greater use to them there. In this way I would fall back on P.S.D. organization to get me exactly where I really wanted to be.

But for a variety of reasons I now rejected this notion. It was partly Tiny, whom I detested, partly the desolate surroundings of the cottage and more particularly the canon himself. The word "evil" I have never used before, because I never knew its meaning until now. The canon was an evil man; no other word will describe him. Even Houseman, traitor and murderer as he undoubtedly was, seemed to feel a deep uneasiness in this sinister presence.

The monster had plainly been detailed to see that I applied myself assiduously to the task in hand. I saw that unless I took immediate steps he would have me at work from morning till night. Like a batsman facing a spin bowler I set about enlarging my territory. I divided the pile of papers into twelve separate groups, labeling them, "First Day," "Second Day," "Third Day," etc., all for the gorilla's benefit. When I had finished the work for the day I wrote a tolerable report and placed it on top of the appropriate heap. Then I resolutely refused to undertake any further work, preferring to spend the late afternoon and evening at my own books and reading the few magazines that had somehow found their way to the cottage.

Of course I could have written any sort of nonsense as far as the canon himself was concerned, but I had a shrewd suspicion that he already might have independent reports on some of the documents. In fact he was probably testing me out. It could well prove suicidal to make a bad assessment of the stuff.

My notion was to lull the gorilla into a false security. I spent the first four days at the cottage. Then on the fifth afternoon I put on my boots and wind jacket, openly declaring my intention of going off for a walk. I never expected that Tiny would allow this, and was amazed that he took no steps to stop me. Always with a cigarette hanging from his lips, he followed on behind.

I made no attempt to hurry, since it was all to my advantage to conceal my true pace. I move fairly quickly on a mountain, especially downhill. It seemed that a very simple plan would suffice to deal with the gorilla. All I had to do was to arrive at the summit of Galtymore, some fifty yards in the lead, and then to set off like the wind down the southern slopes of the mountain.

Things turned out even better than I had hoped for. I reached the top almost 250 yards ahead of the monster. But was the business quite as easy as it seemed? I could have believed that Tiny was simpleton enough to allow me to escape were it not that the canon plainly regarded him as a trustworthy jailer. And the canon knew I had outwitted the Dublin police; he knew of the encounter with Houseman. I decided there must surely be some catch somewhere. Manifestly, I would be well advised to proceed cautiously. The upshot was that I decided to return to the cottage, on the argument that if Tiny were really stupid enough to give me a genuine chance of escape, then he would certainly be stupid enough to give me a second chance.

This was probably the best decision I have ever taken in my life. On the descent back to the cottage I was leading the way by as much as a mile, when from far above there came a shout. Tiny had been unable to restrain himself any longer.

He came down the steepest part of the slope at a pace that I would not have believed possible. Leaping, zigzagging and running, he was down on me in an incredibly short time. He stopped short and then slouched toward me lazily. He hit me a buffet rather than a blow, but it was enough to knock me down. With a stinging head I raged at him, but all he did was to laugh in his maniacal, unnatural fashion. No word was spoken, but I knew it was a bitter disappointment to him that I had not tried to escape.

From now on I strained every wit and nerve on the problem of getting away from Tiny and the cottage. I was hopelessly outclassed in strength and in speed. It was futile to seek a solution along those lines. Two things had to be done: a close scrutiny of the cottage and of the ground outside, and a psychological study of Tiny himself. It had to be a battle between brain and brawn, with the scales heavily weighted in favor of crude muscular power.

Gradually I came to realize that Tiny was possessed of a sly cunning, but of a cunning with definite limitations. There was a car in the garage, as I found in the course of my exploration (which I saw no point in attempting to hide, for the more complex my behavior the harder it would be to distinguish my plan once I had arrived at it). During the evening meal Tiny produced a bunch of keys and a distributor cap. He showed them to me again with his appalling laugh, and then returned them to an inner pocket. So he knew of my discovery of the car, but he could not conceive that I would have any use of it other than its normal function.

At first I thought that only two considerations had any meaning for him: to prevent my escape and to show off his gigantic strength. But there was a third and darker thread to the pattern. Just as I hated his unreasoning power, so he hated me for the things that I was and that he was not. He was hoping that I would try to escape, for then he would have the excuse to pound me to a jelly. He was mortally afraid of the canon, and so did not dare to assault me seriously without reason. Exactly like a cat with a mouse, he continued to give me an apparent chance of escape, just as he had done on the mountain. Like a cat he moved swiftly and astonishingly silently.

I wove my plan from a few gossamer-thin fragments: a length of rubber tubing, a pile of stones where a small object could be concealed, an uncurtained window of the parlor and a couple of empty whiskey bottles. I made my preparations without haste. Everything was ready by the evening of the tenth day, and it seemed that I had still plenty of time to settle my account with the gorilla before the canon should arrive.

But events were to fall out in a vastly more shocking way than anything I could possibly have guessed. By what seemed pernicious ill fortune the monster managed to avoid the one small error that would have finally settled the whole business. Then in the late afternoon of the twelfth day I heard a car coming up the road from the valley. By an equal misfortune the canon was returning two days before time.

Both the monster and I turned out to await the car. This time it was indeed the Chevrolet, now with its original number plates back again. There were four occupants: the canon, Houseman, a man I had not seen before and—Cathleen. They dragged her from the car. As she passed me, on the way to the square concrete building, our eyes met. No word was needed to convey the imploring message of those eyes. This was the "trouble" that Cathleen had spoken of in the bus on the road to Athlone.

The canon was in a false good humor. He seated himself in the cottage parlor with a tumbler of whiskey and proceeded to examine his fingernails while he asked me a series of questions about his precious papers. Tiny lounged against the door. Houseman and the other fellow were preparing supper in the kitchen.

"And now, Mr. Sherwood, to raise a rather different matter. I would be glad to hear the terms of your association with the girl out there." I told him that I knew very little of Cathleen. I told him about our meeting in Longford, about our flight across the bog. There was no harm in this, since it was known to Houseman. I left out all mention of Michael.

The canon still studied his fingers.

"For a young man of your undoubted intelligence, you must realize that this is very unsatisfactory."

"The truth is not always sensational, sir."

Now he looked up with his placid smile. "You know I think I will go over and ask the girl a few questions. She may be able to tell a straighter story."

"She can tell you nothing different, because I have told you the truth."

"Well, well, I shall soon find out. It will do no harm to put a few questions."

Now he smiled. "In fact I shall quite enjoy an interview with such a very charming young lady."

I would readily have made a cheaper bargain with the devil than that of Faustus. I would have asked nothing more than to drive my fists repeatedly into that insincere, smiling face. But Tiny was lounging there within a yard of me.

It was maybe three minutes after the canon had left the room when I heard the first of Cathleen's screams. Tiny lounged against the door, still with a cigarette lightly held between his lips. Every muscle of my body screamed to attack him, but I knew it to be worse than useless. He was simply waiting. His chance had come, and now he would break me. Desperately I looked for some weapon. There was an iron poker in the grate. As if he read my thoughts, Tiny moved away from, not toward, the poker. He wanted me to go for it.

It lasted for perhaps half an hour, perhaps only twenty minutes. The canon returned, his face flushed. The "trouble" had come and gone and I had failed miserably. True, it would have been futile. True, all our chances of escape would have gone. True, I had behaved for the best in the long run. But I had been afraid.

They brought in the supper, and forced me to sit down and eat it with them. I was nauseated as I somehow swallowed the stuff. But I had no alternative, for it was still a little too light outside to suit my purpose.

"I can see you do me a grievous wrong, Mr. Sherwood," said the canon in a rich, winy voice. "You imagine me to be a man who gives way to cheap, vulgar passions."

I made no reply, so he went on. "I do not like my guests to be impolite, Mr. Sherwood." He nodded, and the gorilla came forward to fetch me a vicious slap across the face.

"I fear that is scarcely as refined a gesture as I could have wished," the voice went on. "Not so refined as my own methods, Mr. Sherwood, but no doubt effective for all that."

This was the beginning of the fury that swept through me. The sickness was gone now, replaced by the same cold, shaking fury that had overwhelmed me on the road to Longford. I shivered in spite of the fire behind my back.

"Come, Mr. Sherwood, let me hear you say that you are indeed glad to hear of my restraint. Let me hear you say it!"

Again there came a stinging blow. I must have been very white, and was now trembling quite openly. These symptoms were misinterpreted.

"Tiny! Take the lily-livered poltroon outside before he pukes all over the table."

The monster seized me by the coat, and hauled me violently and roughly from the room.

"Must get to the lavatory," I moaned, twisting somehow free from his grasp.

Once in the open air I made off along the stone pathway that led to the lavatory, the monster padding softly behind. I must explain that twenty yards or so from the cottage there were three upward concrete steps. I took these very quickly, knowing that Tiny would also accelerate his pace. It was now tolerably dark and I had to judge the position of his head by the light from the inevitable cigarette.

As he came up to the last step I unwound my body rather in the style of a discus thrower. My right arm was rigid and horizontal, palm downward. With all the weight of my 160 pounds behind it, and with a madman's added strength, the bony edge of my hand hit him right across the windpipe, a tremendous judo chop. He went down without a sound, for the throat muscles were untensed. Overbalancing, he struck his head a deep, dull blow on the rocky ground. He was quite silent when I reached him. In this he was lucky, for there is not the slightest doubt in my mind that had the wretch been conscious I would have battered him to death on the sharp edge of the steps.

Even as it was I could only restrain the mad rage that consumed me with the greatest difficulty. My hands trembled violently as I sought and found the bunch of keys. Now all I had to do was to create a serious diversion. Then I could release Cathleen, and we could sneak away together in the Chevrolet. And I had just the right means for creating a diversion.

I found my pile of stones and uncovered the two whiskey bottles. They were just as they should be. Then I moved stealthily toward the uncurtained parlor window. When I was some fifteen feet away I flung the first missile with every ounce of strength I could muster. The effect was incredible. The bottle went through the upper left corner, carried clear across the room, bursting on the opposite wall. Petrol was sprayed over the room, some into the fire, and in no more than a second the whole inside was a holocaust. Realizing that this was far more than a diversion, I threw the second. It went clean through the middle of the window. That would be the last cocktail the canon would ever drink.

One of the keys fitted the square concrete building.

"Hello, Deirdre, are you all right in there?"

"Me hands are fastened," she whispered.

The fiend had left her tied across a sort of truckle bed, and it was some minutes before I could free the ropes in the black darkness. From her sobs I realized it would be easier for the girl to recover in body than in mind. She cried out as I rubbed her wrists to bring back the circulation. Then I put my coat around her shoulders and helped her out into the open air.

"Where are they?" she asked.

The cottage was now burning fiercely.

"That's their funeral pyre, my dear."

"You mean he's dead!"

I squeezed her arm. "He won't bother you again for sure."

"Thank God," and I realized with a shock that she meant exactly what she said.

I was anxious to be gone, for there was no sense in delay. The fire might be seen from the valley with possible complications— I had no wish to meet a car ascending the mountain road. It was improbable that the gorilla would recover his senses for many an hour to come, but there was no telling with such a creature.

The electrical circuits on the Chevrolet were new to me, and it wasn't easy to join the right wires— I had no flashlight.

While I fiddled with the thing, Cathleen sat huddled on the front seat. After what seemed an aeon I got the engine started.

I found the mountain road very trying. The automatic transmission seemed to be pulling the car the whole time, instead of serving as a brake down the steep slopes. But, as with like a man restored to prosperity, luck was again on my side. At all events I reached the main road safely.

The next priority was to get away from the immediate neighborhood, and then to get some food for Cathleen. The best thing would be to strike the Cork–Dublin road at Mitchelstown. I hated to do this because of the obvious risk, but there was no alternative, for only on the main road was I likely to find a café or restaurant.

I stopped just outside the small township of Kildorrery. But then I saw by the lights of the large transport café that it would be impossible to take Cathleen inside. Her face was puffed with the ill treatment she had received and her eyes were red. So I brought a substantial pile of sandwiches and a couple of cups of strong coffee out to the car. Cathleen drank the coffee and ate a sandwich under protest.

Luck was again on my side, for we managed another ten miles or so along the main road without being stopped by a patrol car. Then I made a complicated zigzag to the south, through Killavuller and thence onto a smaller road to the west of the Nagles Mountains.

Soon I found a place where the car could be driven off the road into a small wood. This was the right place to stop. We transferred to the spacious back seat and settled down for the night. By a kindly providence we were both dog-tired, and we both managed to get a fair amount of sleep. Toward morning it grew rather cold, so the engine had to be started and the heater switched on. I didn't mind using up the last of the petrol, since I had no thought of taking the car any further.

We ate sandwiches for breakfast by the light of a graying dawn. Cathleen's appetite had improved so markedly that her physical recovery clearly would not be long delayed.

Our destinies were now closely interlinked, so there seemed no point in continuing to hide my real objective.

87

When I had finished my tale she said very simply, "If it is beyond the barrier that you are going, then I will come with you. I am very tired of the life on this side."

We were now perhaps twenty miles from the Boggeragh Mountains, a mere twenty miles from I.C.E. territory. Before we set out I searched through the car and made one important find, a pair of binoculars, which I stuffed into my pocket. Alas, my rucksack was now no more.

So it came about that we set out together over the low hills to the west.

8

FIRST ENCOUNTER WITH I.C.E.

We took the first five miles quite slowly. The ground sloped gently downward toward the Mallow–Cork road. Luckily we struck the road near a point where it was possible to buy simple provisions—bread, cheese, butter, matches and apples. With a bit of string and a modicum of topological ingenuity it was possible to convert my long-sleeved sweater into an impromptu rucksack for carrying the food. It is strange how helpless one feels in wild country without some means of carrying provisions in a more or less effortless way—to attempt carrying in the hands is, of course, useless, and even the capacious pockets of an Irish jacket eventually reach saturation.

By now, Cathleen was walking much more strongly. Even so, it was clear that the journey to the "Barrier" must take two days, fifteen miles the first day, leaving the last five for the second day. In the midafternoon we chanced on a grassy hollow and stopped there for a rest. I was in need of rest, for a reaction from the previous evening was now strongly upon me. Probably for this reason I suddenly had a compelling desire for Cathleen. When I took hold of her she made no protest. But this is really a personal matter, out of place in an intelligence report, so I will say no more of it.

There were two smaller roads, both running roughly north and south, to be negotiated. A couple of miles farther on we found a tumble-down shepherd's hut. It was not an ideal place to spend the night, but at least it did not possess the squalor that a more complete building might have had. The walls were intact up to a height of three feet or so and there was grass on the floor.

While Cathleen collected a pile of heather to lie on, I set about sealing the walls against the wind by plastering the space between the stones with soft turf from the bog. Then we had a great stroke of luck. With the coming of darkness a mist enshrouded the moor. It would now be safe to light a fire. Nearby there was a considerable pile of dry cut turf, of the sort that can be seen everywhere throughout the west of Ireland. Very soon we had a large warming blaze, and we ate a simple, pleasant supper beside it.

The mist stayed down, which was good. It enabled the fire to be kept going throughout the night for one thing. For another, it would now be vastly easier to sneak across into I.C.E. territory. I had abandoned my first idea of crossing during the night with Cathleen. This would be too strenuous. The mist gave us all the advantages of a night crossing anyway.

We pushed along steadily throughout the morning, choosing our route by compass the whole time. The ground rose steadily to a height approaching two thousand feet, which was a sure indication that we were on the crest of the Boggeragh Mountains. By lunchtime I was convinced that we must be across the "Barrier" already.

While we were eating, ragged patches appeared in the mist. At first I didn't realize our incredibly good fortune. It was only when the mist cleared for the second time that I noticed the huge turning aerials. They were about six miles away to the west, mounted on a tongue of high ground to the south of the town of Millstreet. The binoculars taken from the Chevrolet revealed their nature and purpose.

I cursed myself for a fool not to have guessed that I.C.E. would guard its border by radar, in much the same way that the British guarded their island during the late war. Just as we detected the entry of enemy aircraft, so I.C.E. was detecting the entry not simply of aircraft, but of people too. Of course, it was a much harder technical problem to pick out a slowly moving person from a mass of ground reflections, but it was a problem that would easily be within the reach of this fantastic organization.

"I'm sorry, my dear, but we'll have to turn back," I said to Cathleen. "We'll surely be caught if we go on."

When I had explained, she said, "It's to work inside the barrier that I'm going, I care not whether I am caught or no."

"But they'll simply throw you out again, instead of letting you stay and work."

"Knowing what I know, I do not think so."

Looking at her as she then looked, hair fluttering in the same breeze that had blown away the morning mists, I did not think so either. Saint Peter may turn her away from the gates of Heaven, but I do not think so.

"They certainly won't let *me* in, my dear."

"That is likely enough. It would certainly be a great mistake for *you* to go on."

I was too amazed and aghast at the thought of our parting to make any reply.

She took me by the hands. "This is the way of it. Me heart tells me that everything between the two of us is wrong; it was all wrong from the first day." Impulsively she kissed me. "I shall not be forgetting you, Thomas Sherwood. I shall not be forgetting what you did for me back there in the hills."

The capricious mist was down again. In a flash she had darted away and was hidden with an agonizing swiftness. I raced after her but I was too late. I called her name but my voice was choked by the white wall.

With tears in my eyes, I continued to shout her name, running the while in the direction she had gone. Then of an instant I saw that she had the rights of the matter, and like an automaton I turned back toward the east, back in the direction we had come from. A few moments before, we had passed this way together.

The mist was now swirling in patches. Once I had a clear view to the west and thought I could see Cathleen. But I did not turn again, for the case was plainly hopeless. She had the right when she said that everything between us was wrong. On the literal plane I had still thrown away her brother's estate—his wretched manuscript—and I had made no immediate move to save her from the torture of the canon. Back in the hills, the trumpets of Florestan had sounded too late.

Bitterly, I saw that a consistent pattern runs through all the great love stories. The heroine must never be allowed to suffer physical distress; above all the hero must be quite inept. If Orpheus hadn't been an inept ass, if he had recovered his Eurydice, who would have had the slightest interest in their continued marital bliss? Consider the simplicity of good solid muscle men like Naisi and Tristram, tricked by the most transparent devices. Sorrowfully, I realized that my talents were more suited to the city page of the *Times* than to literature or grand opera.

Less remote ideas were crowding into my head. In response to them I put on the most tremendous pace as I ran downhill to the northeast. The sun and wind were fast dissolving the last of the mists.

I heard the helicopter while it was still some way off. I found a space between two boulders and dived into the heather face down. With the lifting of the mist, the pilot was able to come quite low. The noise of his engines rose and fell consistently. I realized that he was systematically sweeping the moor strip by strip.

An intense roar made it plain that the fellow must be hovering almost overhead like some gigantic hawk. I made not the slightest movement. My rough clothing would blend with the heather. Reason told me that my camouflage was excellent. Emotion told me that I would stand out like a sore thumb.

The helicopter moved steadily toward the west. Now I could hear more noises and I knew that there must be more than one of the darned things at work. At length I heard distant shouts and paradoxically I felt a fierce elation. For at last I knew I was dealing with an opponent who was both clever and rational. This was not an organization of bunglers like poor Papa Parsonage. It was not an organization that could be fooled by a pinch of magnesium powder or destroyed by a pint or two of petrol.

The I.C.E. plan was clever and straightforward. As soon as the mist cleared a fleet of helicopters had landed a squad of men who were now scouring the mountainside. The helicopters in the meantime were again aloft and were presumably in communication by radio telephone with the search party. If I attempted to move I would surely be seen from the air and the ground forces would instantly be instructed to pick me up, or off.

Yet the odds were pretty even. It isn't easy to search ten square miles or more of rough ground. And I had one enormous psychological advantage, for I must be outside the main area of the search. From the moment I had reached the eastern slope of the mountain I must have been hidden from the radar scan, and my very swift movement down the eastern flank must be unknown to the searchers. It was rather like looking for a small object in long grass—it becomes very difficult to discover if it lies not quite where one expects.

I lay still and silent, hour by hour, in a dull afternoon sun. Many times I heard voices, and twice there was the sound of boots scraping over the rocks. Probably their owners were at least a hundred yards off, but I could have sworn they were nearer. I did not look up, or behind, as Orpheus would assuredly have done. Cathleen must be caught by now in this finely spun web. I wondered how much she would tell them; probably not too much.

Slowly the day wore on to its close. The light was failing and at last it seemed safe to move. But beyond easing my aching muscles I did not shift from the safe position between the boulders. And it was as well that I maintained caution to the end, for a helicopter came over yet once more, using the very last of the twilight. It was brought home to me that I was dealing not only with a clever and powerful opponent, but with one that was implacable and entirely unrelenting.

The events of the afternoon had settled a point that had

given me cause for worry earlier on. I could not understand why the frontier of I.C.E. territory was so poorly guarded. I had expected to encounter trouble even ten miles or more back from the border. But now I knew why it was made to look so easy: to encourage the unwary into an impossible position. Luck and the mist had saved me.

The advantage lay on my side, however, for I was moving back into practically unguarded country. A forced march through the night would put me beyond the range of the frontier patrols, or at least so I hoped.

The hours of confinement between the boulders had provided an excellent opportunity for putting in some serious thought on this matter of I.C.E. There were three possibilities: to attempt to sneak through the wild areas of moor and mountain; to use the main routes, depending on bluff and trickery; to attack from the sea. I had now satisfied myself that the first alternative was difficult almost to the point of impossibility. Nor had I any confidence in the second. From all I had seen and heard of the I.C.E. it was plain that this particular alternative should be tried only as a last desperate gamble.

So by a process of elimination it followed that I must now explore the chance of a seaward landing into the forbidden area. This at least had the advantage that there was no uncertainty about my next move. I must drive as fast as possible to the northeast, then to the north, swing around Limerick and turn lastly to the west, to the coast of Clare somewhere in the region of Kilkee. There I could contact certain of our agents among the fishermen, agents whose names I had noticed in Colquhoun's notebook.

But all this was still very much in the future. For the present I had a long night's tramp ahead, which was not to be made any more pleasant by the thin, cold rain that started about nine o'clock. I will not attempt to describe the hours of slow walking, again by compass, for there was no moon or stars. It was essential to proceed with great caution. Several times I had to make detours to avoid extensive areas of soft bog. By daybreak I was still five miles or more to the southwest of Mallow.

I was sorely tempted to continue into the town, as I was

now in great need of a hot meal. But this would manifestly be the height of stupidity. My boots and trousers carried certain evidence that I had just crossed the mountains and the marshes. And Mallow would be the first place where they would look for me, if indeed they were looking for me.

Soon I was to find that a search was being prosecuted with great thoroughness. A mile away I gained an extensive view of the main Dublin road, the road that Cathleen and I had driven along two days before. I had not watched for more than a few minutes before I saw that patrols were active everywhere. Cars and buses were being stopped. Every passer-by was being questioned. Possibly I could have crossed the road successfully, but the risk did not seem worth taking. The alternative was to lie up until dark.

My guess is that the search had nothing to do with I.C.E. directly. What presumably had happened was that I.C.E. had contacted the ordinary police, and the police were determined to make a real show of their efficiency.

The day was worse than unpleasant. The rain became heavy and continuous, I had little food left, and I was stiff and cold. Perhaps I should have continued with Cathleen. Perhaps I should have made a genuine offer of my services to I.C.E.

But if I'd taken a job with I.C.E. I would really have been morally bound to drop the whole business, and this I was not prepared to do. It was the intellectual problem, the problem of finding out just what it was that made I.C.E. tick, that was really driving me along. It was the determination to solve this problem that hardened me to withstand the unrelieved misery of the day and of the following night.

The road was crossed safely once darkness had fallen. At first I intended to continue right through until dawn, but a strong cold wind went a long way toward knocking the stuffing out of me. I also crossed the northern road from Cork to Limerick at a point about equidistant between Mallow and Buttevant. About a mile to the west of Doneraile I stumbled on a stretch of woodland. The partial shelter from the wind tempted me to stop for the remainder of the night, it being then nearly three of an appalling summer morning.

In a hollow, well sheltered by trees, I built as large a fire as I dared.

Outside the glow of the fire there was unrelenting blackness. The police, or some curious farmer, or the devil himself for that matter, might be lurking out there preparing to seize me. The wind, shrieking in the trees, sounded like the cries of the damned, and I was insistently reminded that two nights previously I had killed three men.

The rain began heavily again with the coming of dawn. Without food I started out north toward the Ballyhoura Hills. I made no great pace as I struggled over the rough bog. It was well past midday by the time I reached the maze of small roads to the south of Kilmallock. Come what may, I was determined to seek the shelter of some wayside farm.

I had once decided that the right thing to do was to travel through Ireland like a tinker. Now I looked a tinker: wet, grimy, smeared with bog, unkempt. In truth the downpour was now to my advantage, for it provided some excuse for my appearance.

It must have been nigh on three o'clock when I came upon just the right sort of place, near a crossroads.

"Ah!" exclaimed the woman who answered the door, "and it's yourself that looks as if you'd rolled the way through the bog from Kilfinnane."

"My car broke down up on Ballyhourn. I tried to put it right and got all dirty, I'm afraid."

She showed me to a small bedroom. The rain was beating a perpetual cannonade on the window.

"And have you no clothes to put on while your things are dried?"

"I traveled all through the night, Mrs. O'Callaghan, and I'm pretty tired. So I'd be glad of a rest until suppertime. Could you dry my things before then, do you think?"

"By the saints, it's a wonder that you young people do not all come to grief and disaster. But I'll send Paddy up to fetch your clothes in a few minutes' time."

Since she took me for a scatterbrain I decided to play in character.

"I forgot my razor when I left Dublin, and I've had so much

trouble with the old car that I haven't thought about any-thing else."

"So it's a razor you want to borrow. Well, take good care you do not mistake it for your necktie." And she went out with a chuckle.

Quickly I slipped the money out of my trousers and hid it between the blankets, where no doubt it would dry out during the night. It took but a few moments to strip down. Paddy, evidently the husband, collected my dripping garments—is there anything more repulsive than dripping clothes? He left shaving soap, brush and a cutthroat razor. I washed and shaved most gingerly. I was asleep almost before I tumbled into bed.

No more than a second later, it seemed, Paddy was knocking to say that he had brought my clothes and that supper would be ready in a short while.

How good it was to put on warm, dry clothes again. I made the bed carefully because of the money before I went downstairs. A shock awaited me, for it was soon apparent that I had chanced not only on a farm, but on a boarding-house. There were other guests. One indeed was in the hall, taking off oilskins and depositing fishing tackle. He was a small, stocky, humorous-looking man. And he was dressed as a canon of the Church of Ireland.

9

JOURNEY TO THE COAST

All the guests sat down to supper together: the canon, his wife and two children, two rather silent young women schoolteachers and myself.

When the introductions were made I claimed to be a research student in mathematics from Trinity, Dublin not Cambridge. There was no other alternative, for by now it would be nearly hopeless to maintain that I was from England. My accent was an obvious difficulty, but I dealt with this problem by remarking that I had chosen Dublin as a place of study to make easier my intended entry into the services of I.C.E.

The danger of this tactic was that the canon would almost certainly turn out to be a Trinity man himself, and he might trip me with some quite innocently intended question. I deliberately accepted the risk, however, because later on it was possible that I would be obliged to tell the same story to a more searching audience.

But this consideration was irrelevant, for no sooner did I mention I.C.E. than the canon climbed upon a hobbyhorse.

"I would ask you to think very carefully indeed before you take such a step," said he.

I was a little startled by this remark: it was far too reminiscent of the false canon. I took exactly the same line as before, saying that I saw nothing amiss with the activities of I.C.E. But now I received a far more coherent reply.

"Thirty years ago a great world war was fought. And it was fought to suppress just such a regime in Germany as we have here today in Ireland."

"There may be a parallel, sir, between the two cases, but if so I'm afraid it doesn't seem very obvious."

"The parallel is one in which a few men are able to impress their will on the rest. It may be that what is being done now is not the same in detail as it was in Germany a generation ago, but the principle is the same—a few at the top decide what shall be done, and the rest are forced into abject obedience."

The canon's wife kept staring at her husband, as if to stop so dangerous an outflow, but I had no intention of allowing this promising spring to dry up. For here was the first remark I had yet heard that seemed to bear some relevance to the real problem—the driving force behind I.C.E. Not to appear overanxious, I steered the conversation slightly away from the matter in hand.

"I can't quite see why you go back thirty years for an example. Wouldn't the Russians serve the same case?"

The pudding was brought in at this point. Apparently the canon was trying to lose weight, and with this course of the meal of little interest to him, he addressed the table freely.

"A most interesting point," he observed with relish. "The Russian system is no less obnoxious, my dear fellow, but it is subtly different. In Russia, it is the creed itself that dominates; everyone must obey, high and low alike. But here in Ireland it is the high-ups themselves who decide the creed."

"Well, I suppose I must admit that I've never given much thought to who I'd be working for. Are these people at the top of I.C.E. really like Hitler and his gang? I mean personally."

"That I cannot answer, because I've never seen any of these people myself."

"Then . . ."

He interrupted with a wave of his right hand. "How do I know they exist—eh? Well, well, Mr. Sherwood, I've lived in the west of Ireland for almost twenty years. My work brings me into contact with many people, both inside and outside the Church. I saw the first small beginnings of I.C.E. and I've seen it grow step by step over the last ten years."

Now he lifted a finger to emphasize his remark. "And throughout all this time I've never yet come across anyone employed by I.C.E. who really made the important decisions in his own job. They're all slaves, Mr. Sherwood. And that's exactly what I had in mind when I said that you ought to think very carefully before you decide to throw in your lot with these people."

"Then everyone must be acting under instructions, except of course for those who give the instructions. But have you any idea how all this obedience is achieved, sir? It almost sounds like an army."

"It is an army, precisely so. Quite literally, there is a considerable army at work behind the barrier. But I hear darker stories whispered, stories of drugs, even of the use of bacteria. Men are said not to be the same after they have passed through the hands of this I.C.E. medical service."

"Now, John, that's quite enough!" exclaimed his wife. "And at dinnertime too," she added to cover her alarm.

The canon's remarks had a considerable if not profound effect on me. The remark about drugs, although probably guesswork, did fit with Parsonage's statement that I.C.E. somehow managed to take very few agents into its employment. It had always puzzled me how they could take on so many trustworthy scientists (from their point of view) and so few untrustworthy ones. Perhaps this was the explanation. At all events there seemed even less prospect of my being able to bluff myself into the inner councils of this incredible organization.

"But one must agree that the ordinary people of Ireland are much better off now than they used to be," observed one of the teachers.

"One must admit that we are a good deal better off in some directions and a great deal worse off in others," answered the canon.

"There was none of this police surveillance in the good old days," he went on. "No road patrols making endless inquiries, no daytime curfews, no harrying of every stranger in sight."

The teacher silenced, he turned back to me, at last changing the subject. "Paddy tells me that your car is broken down. Tomorrow I'm after going into Limerick for a few hours. Is there anything I can be getting for you?" I thanked him and said that it was a new voltage regulator I would be needing. Then after supper I went along to Mrs. O'Callaghan to ask if I could use the telephone. This done, I rejoined the others in the small sitting room. Meanwhile the storm shrieked across the hillside at the back of the house.

We built up the turf fire in an entirely splendid fashion. Conversation never lagged, for the canon turned out to be a supreme raconteur, with a vast fund of spine-tingling stories. As the evening wore on, he progressed from ghosts seen at third-hand to ghosts seen at second-hand and at last to ghosts that he himself could vouch for upon affidavit. The ladies became decidedly jumpy, and truth to tell I was little better, for the emergence of another canon had been distinctly unnerving. Here he was, telling a sequence of most ingeniously contrived supernatural stories.

It grew so hot in the small room that we opened the door. Still the fire burned brightly, and the rain pelted fiercely on the window. But there came a quite sudden moment of silence, and in that moment I saw from the corner of my eye a streak leap out from the bright-red pile of turf in the grate. In a flash it seemed to cross the room and to be out by the open door. Simultaneously there were piercing screams from the women; the teachers leaped across the room, ending their flight by pinning me completely in the bottom of my chair.

The canon was white about the gills, for I suppose he achieved his skill as a storyteller by half-believing his gruesome yarns. "Now I wonder just what that could be?" he said with a commendable attempt at calm unconcern.

"I wish I could look around a bit," I answered from the depths of my prison. With muttered apologies the schoolteachers removed themselves from the scrummage—their screams had amply compensated for their erstwhile silence.

"It may have been a cat," suggested the canon.

"And how would a cat come to be in the middle of the fire?" countered his wife with implacable logic.

The upshot was that we—the canon and I—went off to consult with Paddy. He assured us that the household kept no cat. In a shaking voice he insisted that it was no cat we had seen but "himself," a view that the canon, with his Protestant tradition, was not disposed to accept. The two of us tramped about the house but we could find nothing. We returned to the sitting room.

"Ah well, it is no matter," remarked the canon with ill-concealed anxiety. "It only shows that we should have been away to bed long ago."

He pulled out a watch and flicked it open. With horror I looked for the imprint of a crown, but there was none that I could see.

The mists of sleep were gathering around me when there was a soft thud on the bed and a subdued miaow. It *had* been a cat, after all.

The wind fell during the night and the rain died to a light

drizzle. The canon was already at breakfast when I came down.

"It *was* a cat," he exclaimed in triumph. "I saw the little beggar on the stairs. It must have been seeking shelter from the storm, got into the chimney somehow and skated down into the room like an Eastern firewalker. Used up half its nine lives at one go, I'm thinking." He laughed uproariously, and one of the teachers smiled rather wanly.

"Doesn't the cat have a very special significance in the practice of witchcraft?" I asked.

No one seemed to have the stomach to pursue this subject. The canon indeed made a sharp turnabout.

"I expect to be leaving for Limerick at about ten o'clock. Would you like to come with me, or can I pick up whatever it is you want?"

I said I would like to go along with him because I wasn't sure of the precise specifications of the voltage regulator, but that I would recognize it when I saw it.

The problem of explaining to Mrs. O'Callaghan that although I would be returning for my car I might not be returning to her house proved a little tricky. Fortunately she still took me for a scatterbrain to be humored. So I managed to pay my due, and the canon and I were away by 10:50 A.M.

About six miles south of Limerick we were stopped at a barrier.

"There's going to be a curfew," remarked the canon with surprising complacency as he brought the car to a stop. A guard handed him a green slip of paper.

"Show this if you should want to go out again, sir. I expect you've got your papers with you?"

"Yes, of course," answered the canon.

"And you, sir?" The question was addressed to me.

"Yes, of course," I replied.

The car picked up speed, and I was now trapped in a city under a daytime curfew where all strangers were hunted on sight. Not for the first time I deplored my lack of Irish identification papers. I had not wished to carry such papers through the Dublin immigration—and Seamus Colquhoun had been a broken reed. My British passport would be a sadly inadequate document. The bad error had been to accompany the canon, but the lift to Limerick was nearly halfway to my destination, and after the long miserable tramps of the preceding days I had allowed myself to be seduced by his offer.

The canon dropped me in the city, saying that he would meet me at about four, outside the Hilton Hotel. I was sorry not to be able to say good-by, for I had no intention of being outside the Hilton Hotel at four.

Without delay I sought out the Pan American Airways office.

"I phoned yesterday, booking an evening flight to London," I said to the clerk.

"What name, sir?"

"Sherwood, Thomas Sherwood."

He looked through his list, and then nodded in confirmation. "Could I see your passport, please?"

The misgiving I felt in handing it over was tempered by the realization that if I couldn't deceive an airline clerk my case would indeed be hopeless. He glanced at the photograph, ripped a counterfoil off my visa and handed the passport back. I suppose it must have seemed very natural that someone with a British passport should be booking a flight to London.

He filled out a ticket and handed me a green boarding card. I paid for the ticket and said, "I noticed that you gave the fellow before me a yellow boarding card. Why was that?"

The clerk dropped his voice. "We're instructed by the police to issue yellow cards to anyone who books a flight *after* a curfew is announced. You'll be all right with your card, sir. If I may give you a bit of advice I'd take an early bus out to the airport."

"Why?"

"Because the police like everyone with valid papers to get out of the city as soon as possible. That makes it easier for them to deal with the rest."

I climbed into the bus, thanking my lucky stars that by some sixth sense I'd had the wit to make a booking by phone the previous night. Almost the worst that could now happen was that I should find myself back in London. I hadn't really fulfilled my mission, but at least I'd have a tolerable story to tell. At all events I could make things a bit easier for anyone who should follow me.

It was probable that the police would notice that I was seriously offbeat, as far as my itinerary was concerned at any rate. It was possible that I'd be held for questioning, but I couldn't see that any serious charge could be sustained against me. If they had grounds for really strong suspicion, then by good detective work there was little doubt that the whole course of my activities could be reconstructed, but there wasn't the slightest reason why they should go to such lengths. The most likely thing was that I'd be kept under close watch until I boarded the plane—that I wouldn't be allowed to slip away at Shannon Airport.

But I was saved by my companion in the bus. He was a little man, I should judge of maybe sixty-five, dressed in a blue wind jacket that boasted the insignia of the New Jersey Snow Club. He told me that he was a small manufacturer from the town of Elizabeth, on his first visit to Ireland. When the police boarded the bus and were looking through the papers of the people in front of us, he began deploring this undemocratic activity in a loud voice. The police kept glancing at us, and heads were constantly being turned. Then the little fellow announced, "And what's more, I haven't even been allowed to see anything of this I.C.E. business. From all I hear they've quite a few things that we could make use of back home in the States."

When the police reached us, he scowled at them. "Always hustling innocent people about. I'll have a few questions to ask when I get back to New Jersey."

In their anxiety to get at the old fellow, the guards somewhat naturally were rather superficial in their examination of my things. My green card, passport and visa stamp were all they bothered with.

But they put the old chap's effects through a fine toothcomb, luggage and all. He never ceased to complain the whole while. He would write to his representative in Congress. He would get his wife to complain to the local woman's club, a threat which two other male Americans assured the guards to be serious. The police retired at last, baffled men.

I had the impression that I wasn't the only person in the bus to sigh with relief.

I was not averse to visiting the airport. On the face of it the easiest way into I.C.E. territory would be to land at the airport and then to take a small boat down the Shannon, eventually landing somewhere on the south bank. Quite apart from espionage, it was certain that profitable smuggling of I.C.E. products must be taking place through the airport. I once read the precept that wherever an economically profitable racket exists, it is a certainty that such a racket will receive full exploitation. If so, there surely had to be a route through Shannon Airport into I.C.E. land.

Manifestly I should learn little from hanging about the main lounge, and it would be unwise to go roaming about the airfield until I knew the layout better. I had once worked for a month during the summer at a Strathpeffer Hotel, spending my earnings afterward in climbing the Northwestern Highlands, so I had some slight knowledge of kitchen and restaurant work. I knew that there are always cleaning jobs that no one likes to do, and I resolved to present myself as a new recruit for one of these jobs. I looked the part, something of a ruffian, and I knew that my credentials would not be overanxiously surveyed. I knew also that it was unlikely that I would be given any job that brought me into contact with the public. Such jobs are always sought after, because of the chance of tips. It was unlikely therefore that I would run any risk of recognition by my companions in the bus.

I had a few suitably grimy sheets of paper taken from the Unicorn Hotel in my pocket. On one of them I scrawled the following ludicrous message:

This is a recommendation for Joe McCloy. He is a good man to have around.

SHAUN HOUSEMAN

MANAGER

As I expected, the kitchen manager gave me a job. It was also the sort of job that I expected, and I set about it with the expected measure of inefficiency.

The time of my flight came and went, which gave me a

rather greater degree of freedom. They might be looking for Thomas Sherwood, the precise, pedantic student, back in there, but they wouldn't notice rough, tough Joe McCloy unloading supplies outside the kitchen door.

I struck up the acquaintance of a boilerman with the improbable name of Rory Parnell, and as he was able to find me very rough sleeping quarters I decided to stay on for a while in my new guise. I bought shaving equipment, a cake of soap and a clean shirt, the latter a villainous green-check affair that looked quite the part.

It was three days later, sometime after ten o'clock in the evening, when one of the waiters in the lounge pulled me aside.

"Joey, me bhoy," says he, "I'm after getting away for a few hours. I'm asking you to take me place like a true friend."

Since this was the first time we had spoken together it was hardly clear how I came to be his true friend, but nothing abashed he went on.

"And it's only a few wee orders for tea and coffee that you'll be getting, and maybe an odd glass of whiskey. And it's the tips you'll be pocketing."

I acted the part of wooden obstinacy to the point of stupidity, and only when the fellow had offered quite a considerable bribe did I accede. Either he was engaged on some nefarious activity or he was visiting a girl; so much was clear from the size of the bribe. I put on his white jacket and took over.

The job was of course quite easy. Each new flight brought in a fresh crop of customers. In the abstract, I was surprised to see how much in the way of tips I was beginning to accumulate. No wonder these jobs were sought after, and no wonder their holders soon developed a bland and debonair confidence.

I imagine it must have been about 2:30 A.M. when I noticed a lone man signaling me from an alcove. I went over to take his order. Our eyes met, and I saw it was the New Jersey Snowman, but now without his wind jacket.

"And so we meet again, young fellow. Would you be good enough to step outside? I've a proposition to make and I don't want to be overheard by every busybody."

When we had found a quiet spot he went on. "If they think Hiram Q. Savage is going to be beaten by all these rules and regulations, well, they're going to learn something different, doggone it. I said I would see this I.C.E. and see it I will. I don't aim to become a laughingstock back home in Elizabeth, no sir! But I'll need your help, young fellow."

"How can I help?"

"This is the deal. I have a boat all ready, moored in the river, right near here. I was mortified when I learned that I couldn't use a motored craft because of the noise, and I'm too old now to row very far."

"So you want me to row you across the river?"

"Right. Maybe I ought to say that I've got an idea that you aren't quite what you claim to be. Maybe I ought to go right back in there and tell 'em what I think. But I won't. I'll make you a fair offer instead."

We haggled for a few minutes, and in the end he offered me fifty Irish pounds to land him into I.C.E. territory. Two things were plain: one that he was very innocent and the other that he must want to get through the barrier rather badly if he was willing to risk a hazardous river trip. For I had no doubt that, quite apart from the patrols that must be operating on the river, it would be a risky business to try crossing the currents of the Shannon during the night hours in a small boat.

Of course he might be an *agent provocateur* but I thought the chance sufficiently slight; it would be worth while following his proposal a little further. My idea was to use his boat, not to cross the Shannon at all but to cross the wide mouth of the river Fergus. This would save a long detour by land. If I could get ashore in the neighborhood of Kildysart, it would only be an easy day's walk into Kilkee.

"How do you know I won't go back in there and tell 'em about you?" I asked.

"When a man has lived as long as I have, and when he's done as much business as I have, he learns to be some judge of character. Either he learns or he goes out of business, and I'm not out of business yet."

"How did you get hold of this boat?"

"And he learns not to give his friends away. Don't forget that, young man."

"Very well. Let me see your boat."

I cached my white overall; it was obviously too conspicuous. We skirted the airfield, the little man leading the way with the sprightliness of a gnome. At length we reached the east–west channel that separates the mainland from an island to the north. Instead of a waiting posse of guards there was indeed a small boat moored near the western end of the channel. The oars I noticed were muffled. I reckoned it would be reasonably safe to assay the crossing of the Fergus estuary. This opinion was backed, I might say, by an extensive experience in the VIIth eight of the First and Third Trinity Boat Club.

There was no moon but sufficient starlight for me to have a clear view of my passenger as I sculled out from the shore. I saw him take a round instrument from his pocket, which I realized must be a compass.

"You're far too much to the west. Turn to my left until I give you the word to stop."

Of course I was keeping to the west as closely as I could judge from the stars. I followed my original course without deviation.

Now he pulled a second instrument from his pocket, however. I caught a glint of starlight on it and knew it for a revolver.

"There will be no nonsense. Turn the boat as I tell you." Once again I realized that I had blundered.

I set the boat on its new course, and said, "You realize that what you're trying to do is extremely risky."

"Of course I realize it," he answered with scorn.

"But it's mad. It means going through Tarbert race."

"Of course it does, but the tide will be in our favor, if you get ahead and don't talk so much. Come on, take her along faster."

"You're welcome to try if you think you can do better. I tell you it's crazy. There must be some easier way of getting into I.C.E. territory."

"If there is I haven't found it, and I've been trying for a long time."

"That doesn't justify such an extreme risk."

"In my case it does. I'm an old man without many more years to live. If I were in your position, young fellow, I might of course think differently."

"I do think differently."

"But you aren't doing the thinking," he answered with a chuckle.

Would he shoot if I changed course? Probably the risk was about the same as the risk from the river. If we made the trip to the I.C.E. shore I should be where I wanted to be. So on balance it was probably best to head downriver, but I didn't like the way the current was already beginning to grip the boat.

"Surely you weren't relying on a chance encounter to provide someone to row for you on this trip?" I remarked out of curiosity.

"Surely I was not," he replied. "The young man whose job you had taken at the airport contracted to accompany me. He received a considerable payment on account, so that when he refused to make good the bargain I was obliged unfortunately to deal rather severely with him."

"And how did you decide to put your proposition to me?" Again the chuckle. By now the boat was moving at a fair pace, and the water was getting a bit heavy.

"I knew you were compromised. I guessed it already in the bus."

"Then I have you to thank for what you did. I'll repay you by offering a piece of good advice." I paused to readjust the boat, which seemed to have been pushed somewhat off course.

"And what is that?" he asked.

"Get rid of the pistol. In my experience pistols always cause trouble for their owners."

Again he laughed. "Well, well, we shall see."

It was now high time to stop talking, to give all my attention to the boat. We were approaching the main stream of the Shannon and there were a number of islands on the westward flank. We rounded them successfully and began to move downriver. I kept the boat on the northern side, for I wanted to avoid the central current as long as possible.

The tug of the current was indeed now very obvious, and I think we must have been approaching Foynes when a bright light flared up quite close to us. It was the searchlight of a patrol boat lighting up, not our little craft, but a larger one with a whole group of people—maybe six—in it. I recovered my wits quicker than the old fellow and in a flash I brought the blade of one of the oars across the hand that held the gun. Luckily it was knocked into the water without going off.

In an instant I turned the boat and pulled hard toward the northern shore.

It was a long grinding struggle but I made it by the first faint light of dawn. I was pretty spent and the old chap was moaning that I had broken one of his fingers. Crossly I waded through shallow water and brought the boat into land. As I helped him out I remarked, "There was never any chance of getting through that way. Don't you realize that the whole river is endlessly patrolled and that those boats are equipped with radar? And for another thing, I told you it was unlucky to carry a gun."

I fixed up the old fellow's hand as best I could—it wasn't seriously damaged—and got him onto the road for Kildysart. As soon as I decently could I stopped at a small farm for breakfast.

Although this improved me a great deal, I was pretty tired, partly from the long row and partly from walking with wet feet. I was therefore quite pleased to see a motorist at work on his car—this was perhaps five miles from Kilrush.

"Can I give a hand?" I asked.

There was something vaguely familiar about this motorist. He was peering into the engine and he now looked up at me. The shock of seeing Houseman and the false canon together on that fateful morning back at Slievenamuck had been no greater than this. The true canon's belief in ghosts was vindicated. For here was none other than Seamus Colquhoun.

10

BEYOND THE BARRIER

"Well, well, Mr. Colquhoun. And how does it feel to be raised from the dead?"

"So it's Mister Sure-fire, trying to be funny."

Of course the report in the *Irish Times* hadn't mentioned Colquhoun by name. I had simply jumped to what seemed a reasonable conclusion. I did what I could by way of explanation.

"Now isn't that just like Mr. Clever-Dick?" he said. "Was there nobody but meself in the whole of Dublin on whom the guards might be wanting to set a hand?"

"The time and place seemed singularly appropriate."

"They did, did they?"

Colquhoun rose threateningly, a wrench in his right fist.

"And where would the notebook now be?" he asked.

"With Mr. Houseman of the Unicorn Hotel, Longford, of course."

"You shrunken pin-wit," he roared, "you should have found out that the man was sold to the divil."

"As a matter of fact I did find out, but orders are orders. Mine but to do and die, you know."

"You'll be dead before your time," he growled, taking a step toward me.

"Quit fooling, Colquhoun. If you don't drop that spanner I'll knock all Hades out of you. When I found Houseman had thrown in his lot with the P.S.D. crew, I burned the book. It's fertilizing some farmer's field."

He put down the wrench and leaned against the car. "Is that the truth of it?"

"Of course."

"What a shocking pity you didn't keep it!"

"Stop being a pinhead yourself. I might have been caught half a dozen times these last three weeks. Did you want the police to get hold of the damned thing?"

"No, I suppose for an amateur you did the best you could," he conceded.

"What news do you hear of Houseman?"

"The best," he answered. "There is a good chance that he may have departed from this vale of tears."

"How did you come to hear that? I had quite a bit of trouble with the man."

"Listen to little Mr. Wren, the King of Birds. Listen to him sing! He had trouble with the man!"

"It looks as if you'll be having quite a walk, Mr. Colquhoun, unless you can get your car running again."

"It's a strange tale. A horrible huge mountain of a fellow appeared one day in the town of Tipperary with a cracked skull."

"Which strikes me as one of the most unlikely statements I've ever heard."

"I'm after telling you again, and for the last time, not to be always interrupting me. As I was saying, this horrible fellow appears in Tipperary with multiple fractures of the cranium. What makes this such a noteworthy incident is that this same fellow is known to be bodyguard of the moguls of P.S.D."

"Which doesn't seem to me to make the story any more probable. Surely you can see that for yourself?"

Colquhoun was now getting thoroughly angry. But he plowed determinedly on. "A strange tale this fellow tells when at last they get him to talk."

"Who gets him to talk?"

"The guards, of course. Then up they went to a high mountain farm, where they found a most terrible scene, a scene of shocking debauchery. Apparently the whole party was carousing and became so drunk that the place was set

111

on fire, and all were burned to ashes before anyone could notice the approach of death."

"Colquhoun, you're a grammarian's nightmare. Don't you think it would be a little more profitable if we were to get the car started? Was Houseman one of the party?"

"That is not known for certain, but it is my belief that he was. Little was found to identify the divil's party, except this."

I could not restrain a cry of astonishment. The object Colquhoun held in his hand was a portion of a watch. The metal had partially melted, but an imprint of a crown could still be distinguished. Colquhoun clicked his tongue in a deprecating fashion.

"What would you do without your nursemaid, little feller?" he said. "I had to remove the metal frame of a rucksack from that fire, one that was made in England. The guards might have been a wee bit curious about that rucksack."

He roared with laughter, for I suppose I looked uncommonly like a stuck pig.

"But . . ." I began.

"How did I find out? Your young lady friend, of course, Mr. Know-it-all. She got in touch with me after that business back at Longford. Unfortunately she wouldn't wait to have me join her before she was after trying to hit Houseman for six, and got herself caught for her pains. I had to follow on several days behind, but I kept your trail all right."

"Did you expect me to head in this direction?"

"Don't flatter yourself that I'm consumed with interest about what you may be doing, although I'll allow that I'm a bit curious to know how you managed to split that feller's headpiece."

"And I suppose you know what happened to Cathleen?"

"She's gone to take her brother's place behind the barrier. And would there by anything else you might want to know, me infant prodigy?"

Was this possible? Did these people spend the whole of their lives living some part or other?

"I suppose you're trying to pull together the remnants of your scattered organization?" I asked.

"And by what might mental process did you arrive at that conclusion?"

"I didn't, I'm asking."

"Then you may ask."

I moved over to the car, and asked, "What's wrong?"

"The engine isn't firing properly."

"I'll bet it isn't, and not only the engine if you ask me."

"I'm not asking," grunted Colquhoun, waggling his spanner in a hopeless fashion.

I got to work on the machine. Some minutes later I straightened my back, now rather stiff from the rowing, and said, "It's no use, your voltage regulator has gone."

"What does that mean, Jacko?"

"It means that you'll have to get a new one and get your battery charged; it's hopelessly flat. And it means you'll have to walk. Got any dry socks?"

"What should I be wanting dry socks for?"

"You're not, it's me that's wanting 'em."

Colquhoun complained so strenuously throughout the walk into Kilkee that his sentiments became quite contagious. In spite of the socks, I was quite tired by the time we arrived there. During the last mile or so my companion became silent, however. With complete assurance he strode into the little fishing port. Although to my eye an incongruous figure, he seemed to attract no notice as we walked through the groups of men and animals that thronged the streets. An occasional lorry or car hooted its way through the melee. This was plainly the Ireland of old. Only a few miles to the south, across the estuary of the Shannon, lay the most modern industrial development that the world had yet seen.

Colquhoun turned down a side street, took a crooked path to avoid dogs lying on the pavement, and stepped inside an open door. Although I didn't realize it explicitly, I must have allowed him to take the lead, for I followed him without question. It never occurred to me that the guards might be waiting for us.

They were not, but our entrance into the house nevertheless had a small touch of drama about it. A powerfully built, dark-haired young fellow, obviously a fisherman, was at a very late breakfast. A good-looking girl seemed busily engaged at a fireside oven. We were greeted with looks that might possibly be translated into these words: "The past is back to haunt us. Dear God, must we go on being persecuted forever just because we were once foolish enough to make a small wee mistake?" Manifestly, Colquhoun and I were not welcome.

I took no immediate part in the following conversation, which at the same time proved to be both animated and disjointed. Stripped of the unnecessary verbiage that appeared to be inseparable from any talk with Colquhoun, the situation was plainly that Mike and Mary O'Dwyer—husband and wife —had worked for Colquhoun in the past, but now were anxious to break an embarrassing association. Indeed they had been hoping until our arrival that the connection had come to an end in a natural way with the disintegration of Colquhoun's band. Colquhoun for his part was anxious to reforge his chain, and O'Dwyer was a necessary link, for it appeared that O'Dwyer was the acknowledged expert at getting agents into I.C.E. territory. In short, O'Dwyer was exactly my man.

It wasn't difficult to understand O'Dwyer's point of view. He owned his boat, and there was a ready market to the south for all the products of legitimate fishing. He could be entirely prosperous without risk. Indeed it was obscure why he had ever become involved with Colquhoun in the first place. Maybe that was how he came to own the boat, or maybe it was the excitement.

At all events, the excitement had no appeal now for O'Dwyer.

"I tell you it just cannot be done, Mr. Colquhoun," he exclaimed repeatedly. "It's not like the old days when I could take the boat into any beach or cove. Every place is now watched by electric waves. Even at night, the patrol boats are able to hunt down anybody who comes within five miles of the shore. And there are submarine nets across all the bays, so that underneath the water there is no way either."

I thought it time to join in. "This is all true except in heavy weather. When the sea waves are high they reflect the radio transmission like a whole mass of little ships. Then it's quite impossible to separate a true ship from the sea waves. That's why an attempt from the sea is much more likely to succeed than one from the land—always provided it's made in bad weather."

"Is it that you're after supporting his argument?" exclaimed Colquhoun.

I felt that much more of this sort of remark would drive me straight to the madhouse, for one simply could not discuss any question with Colquhoun in a normal way.

"I'm not supporting and I'm not denying an argument," I exclaimed with some exasperation. "I'm not concerned with argument. I'm *telling* you what the situation is."

Mary O'Dwyer set an appetizing plateful in front of me, and I realized that at any rate a part of my irritation was probably due to hunger.

"Maybe what you say is right enough," said Mike, drinking tea from a large mug between his words. "But who is to take a boat in heavy weather into such a coast? Nobody but a madman, I'm thinking."

"Could you manage to carry a small motorboat without its being seen?" I asked.

"It might be done."

"Then there's one way in which the business could possibly be managed. Instead of carrying a passenger right in to the coast, you might set him down at sea in the motorboat, maybe four miles or so out. Then you would simply leave it to the passenger to find his own way safely."

O'Dwyer looked curiously at me. "All very fine, except for one thing."

"And what's that?"

"The sea. Do you know what bad weather on the Irish Coast is like? Two winters ago a lighthouse keeper was drowned, washed by a wave off the rocks at a place certainly 150 feet above the normal sea level."

"Then we're talking at cross-purposes. I'm not asking for a storm, with waves fifty feet or more in height. Waves of about fifteen feet would hide an ordinary fishing boat from the I.C.E. radar. Waves of as little as six feet would hide a small motorboat."

O'Dwyer was still not convinced.

"It would be very risky for a stranger in a small boat to attempt a night landing, even with the sea calm."

"*You* wouldn't be taking the risk."

"That is true, but I see the danger. And where would I be getting the motorboats? Every time a new one would be needed."

"That's Colquhoun's business. If he wants your help, he ought to supply the equipment."

"And isn't it nice," Colquhoun broke in, "for me to have me affairs all fixed and decided by a young cock sparrer? So I'm to supply the equipment, am I? And what are you going to supply, Mr. Smart-Wits?"

"I'm going to take the risk. If you'll get the motorboat, and if Mike will take it on, I'll undertake to see whether this business can be managed or not."

"And now I know how a toy soldier gives his orders, just like little Mr. Twopence-Ha'penny here."

I don't often lose my temper, but now I quickly leaned across the table and banged the inner edge of Colquhoun's plate with my fist. The plate rose, turned over in the air and deposited the food down the front of his suit.

"If you'd really like to learn how I split that fellow's skull, I'd be happy to give a demonstration," I said.

Colquhoun's dislike of me was, I thought, the dislike of the professional for a cocky amateur. And he was smarting sufficiently under recent reverses to be glad of some show-down that he might hope to win, for I had no doubt he was pretty handy with a knife. But O'Dwyer gave him no chance.

"I'll have no brawling in the house," O'Dwyer roared. He was big and active enough to beat the daylights out of the pair of us, and I couldn't help wondering why Colquhoun's sudden appearance had disturbed him in the least degree. How does an Intelligence Service keep its agents?—through the fear of being denounced?

I stood up to go.

"Thank you very much for the meal, Mrs. O'Dwyer. I'm sorry I made such poor use of some of your food."

"And where would Mr. Suck-and-Blow be going?"

"To buy a couple of pairs of socks," I answered, biting back an obvious retort.

I bought the socks and a bag of apples, which I munched strolling about the pier looking over the fishing boats. Except for riding a real storm they appeared eminently seaworthy. There was a seat against the sea wall. Before I realized it I was asleep in the sun. A somewhat unkempt figure placidly snoozing would hardly excite any grave suspicion in the breasts of the local constabulary, not in this corner of Old Ireland, with its mingled scent of fish and horses.

I revived some three hours later, feeling that I needed to stick my head under a water tap. The first thing to do, I thought as I strolled back along the pier, was to get a job on one of these boats; not likely to be much difficulty in that, because there was a shortage of labor everywhere, so much was being absorbed by the industry to the south. Perhaps I should try O'Dwyer first. At least there'd be no danger of him giving me away to the police. In any case I must return to his home to pick up my things.

When I got back to the O'Dwyer home I found that Colquhoun had left—an indescribable relief, for I was really very tired indeed, what with only one proper night's sleep in an extremely trying week. It worried me out of proportion that I couldn't return the socks.

"Would you be needing a new hand, Mike?" I asked.

"And what would I give out about ye?"

"That I'm a student from Dublin, working on a summer job for a few weeks. Name, Thomas Sherwood."

"How d'ye do, Tom me bhoy. Any experience?"

"Very little, I'm afraid; a few trips out from Bideford."

"Well, well, that will not be unlike a student from Dublin," he said with a chuckle.

"Old Slugeamus has a spare room where ye can sleep. Ye can trust him with the life of ye. I'll be after showing you the way to his cottage."

"Ah, he cannot go there," objected Mary O'Dwyer. "They say the flies is as big as bees around his cottage."

"Away with ye, woman. He'll be as right as rain," answered Mike.

Seamus McCarthy, known as "Old Slugeamus," turned out to be a more or less permanent member of O'Dwyer's crew, a fellow who managed to fish all night and drink all day in a most amazing fashion. At first I thought that he never slept, but later I discovered that even in sleep he did things to excess. When the weather was bad, he would often sleep the clock around, twice. His cottage was in indescribable confusion, a pulsating scene to which a vociferous parrot made due contribution. In the two weeks I spent at Kilkee I managed to get no more than a superficial semblance of order into the place. In any case I suspect that the task would have proved rather like painting the Forth Bridge: that a stage would have been reached where Slugeamus spread wreckage and destruction as fast as I was able to establish order. This stage was never reached, Slugeamus always being several orders of magnitude ahead of me.

In appearance he was fairly tall, stoutish, sandy-haired, with complexion to match. He wore a huge black sweater, rubber boots and a cap. I suppose he had a shirt too, but I never saw it, since the roll of the sweater came high on a short neck.

I must have made a great hit with him. One evening, in his cups, he produced a small waterproof canister.

"Taken from a stiff," he announced proudly.

"Who, what, and where was this stiff?"

"Santa Maria, hear him talk, like a powerful great book. This feller was all swelled up by the sea, been bobbing and floating out there a dozen Masses, no less."

"He means that the corpus had been afloat for nigh on two weeks," translated O'Dwyer.

"Bobbing like a wee porpoise between the rocks," agreed Slugeamus, "grampus-like."

"And what was in the canister?" I asked.

"Aren't we waiting to hear what the professor has to say?" This seemed a cue, so I managed to open up the thing. Inside was a small roll of paper. Written on it was a short cryptic message:

.*Twin helices. Senses opposite.*

The only twin helices I could think of were the helices of the Crick-Watson theory of DNA. But why should a "corpus" be bobbing around the ocean carrying a message that related to the structure of nucleic acid? In any case the statement

118

"Senses opposite" was obscure. This seemed to be just another of those minor mysteries of life that one is not destined to solve. But in thinking so I was wrong.

After the shocking weather of the previous week it would have been reasonable to expect heavy seas. Perversely, day after day was now fine and the sea quite calm. The rhythm of a new life became established. We would leave port about an hour before sundown, the boat driven by a powerful diesel engine. Looking back toward the land, the whole bay would seem to be overflowing, like a blue basin filled to the rim.

So we would throb our way out toward the great glowing red ball that hung low in the western sky. I would look assiduously for the "green flash" at the last moment of the declining sun, but never with certain success. Then would come the casting of the net and the inspection of lobster pots. Strange that our modern industrial civilization seems to have contributed so little to the technique of fishing. The locomotion of the boat is modern, of course, but the actual method of fishing is unchanged.

During the night we would cook some succulent fish, or a lobster, which we would wash down with mugs of tea, our digestions being good. After dawn the net would be taken in, and the fish sorted into boxes during the journey back to port. Back at the jetty would come the handling of the boxes on the quay and into a waiting lorry. And on occasion the net would have to be mended, an art in which I was instructed by Slugeamus. I don't think that I could ever match the deft swiftness of his fingers, even if I were to practice for a generation.

But it was easy to see how the method of handling the boxes might be improved. It seemed possible to mount a temporary derrick on one of the masts, and then to use a pulley block to lift the boxes directly from the hold of the boat onto the back of the lorry. I mentioned the idea to Mike O'Dwyer.

"Aye, that's the way of the Picts. But how would it be worth while with a catch as small as ours?"

"But there's every reason to be thinking of increasing your catch now that there's no lack of a market."

"And that's true enough," he agreed.

It came about that there was never any opportunity to put this idea into practice, however. One day Mike showed me a small motorboat about ten feet long, well designed to avoid flooding of the engine by breaking waves. I concealed my curiosity as to where the new boat had come from, for I had no real doubt that it was a peace offering from Colquhoun. Without unnecessary discussion I spent a couple of afternoons taking down and reassembling the motor. Although I would have dearly liked to make a few trips into the bay, it would have been manifestly foolish to advertise either the boat or myself unduly.

Shortly afterward we had news on the radio of heavy weather blowing up from the southwest. There were only three other boats that put out along with us on the fateful night. The rain was falling and the quay was almost deserted, so that Mike decided very simply to tow the little craft behind us. Even so it did not entirely escape notice. A jibe from another crew was met by Slugeamus.

"What should it be, me bhoy, but our lifeboat?"

I hoped that he had the rights of the matter.

Our plan was simple. A glance at any map of Kerry will show that a boat may be taken well into Dingle Bay without ever coming within five miles of the shore. Somewhere south of Dingle the motorboat would be released, and I would head on a northeast course, using the sea and the wind to set me on the northern shore of the bay, a shore mainly without cliffs.

The trip was a very long one for O'Dwyer, almost one hundred miles each way. Reckoning on a maxium speed of twelve knots, this meant at least sixteen hours of continuous pounding, even if the weather got no worse. It meant that he couldn't hope to regain the shelter of Kilkee harbor until ten or eleven the following morning. I mention this to exonerate O'Dwyer from all reasonable blame for the events that were to follow.

The weather worsened. We were now south of the Shannon, somewhere on ten miles to the seaward of Kerry Head. It was a difficult decision. Should we turn back, or should we go on, now that we were so close? We decided to go on, O'Dwyer declaring that he would have the sea and wind with him on the return—and if a storm should be blowing up he would run for Dingle. The crew would then of course be arrested, but on a fair claim of bad weather he would surely be eventually escorted back to waters north of the Shannon. In the latter case I would leave the trawler and head for the south side of Dingle Bay.

About three in the morning O'Dwyer at last decided that the moment of parting had arrived. He also declared that he would attempt to return by the way we had come. Slugeamus put a wet arm around me. "Let's hope we shall not be weeping for you," he shouted.

The sea was heaving most unpleasantly. We pulled the little motorboat in as near as we dared. By the light of an electric torch it seemed nearly impossible to board her. One moment she lay in the trough of a wave, the next halfway up the trawler's side. But this was the moment I had been asking for, so there was no use fussing. The thing to do was to jump when the boat was at its highest.

I tied a rope about my waist in the fashion of a mountaineer —I did not wish to be too encumbered by a life belt. O'Dwyer was at the wheel, attempting to keep the best distance between the trawler and the motorboat. So I gave the rope to Slugeamus, making sure that there was the right amount of slack. Then I stood, flashlight in hand, watching the boat coming up, down, up, down, up again for the last time, and I jumped. Painfully I moved my arms and legs in turn to make sure that I was only bruised.

As soon as they saw I was safely in and able to move, O'Dwyer allowed the distance between the craft to increase, but he didn't give the order to cast off until I had the engine started, which in my cold, numbed state took quite a while.

The little vessel bobbed like a cork. No radar could detect me, at least that much was quite certain. It was essential to run the engine slowly, so I concentrated simply on maintaining direction—the gathering storm from the southwest would drive me in, for I felt sure now that a storm was coming.

I steered by compass pretty well to the north, rather than

to the northeast, since I felt that the sooner I got away from the middle of Dingle Bay the better. There can be no doubt that I owe my life to this slight change of plan.

No words can describe the stark horror that can be compressed into a single moment of time, so I shall not attempt any gaudy description. The plain facts are that I was cold, bruised, soaked to the skin, sick from the motion of the boat, when after an hour or more I heard above the wind the sound of waves breaking ahead. Nor was it the sound of waves breaking on a beach, but the roar of great waves hitting the base of a high cliff.

There was nothing to be done but to turn about and to give the engine full throttle. With the thought that O'Dwyer had taken me too far in and that I must be somewhere in the region of Anascaul, I turned to the west. Now I was side-on to the waves and it was only a question of time before the engine would be swamped.

With the feeling that all was surely finished, and that O'Dwyer had given me fair warning, I now concentrated only on finding calmer water and on keeping away from the cliffs. I suddenly realized to my surprise that the engine was still firing and that the motion of the boat was distinctly less. Checking on my compass I found I was heading south-southwest, out to sea again! I was too confused to perceive the true explanation of this singular situation. I knew only that every minute was carrying me into calmer water.

The night was intensely black and I had no warning, except perhaps the clearer note of the engine. The boat struck hard against a rock. I was too shaken to make a move, and it wasn't until the heaving sea had taken the vessel off and then impaled it for a second time that I made a frenzied leap for safety. I kicked furiously, banged my knees and tore my nails, and at last found myself on a rock ledge with the water sucking below.

Slowly I edged up the rocky wall. If I could climb ten feet or more I might be safe from a rising tide. Soon I found myself crawling rather than climbing. A few moments later I felt grass under my hands. Evidently I had reached the flat top of some small rocky outcrop. I continued to crawl until the noise of the sea became muffled. Then I lay down, exhausted, to wait for dawn.

Dawn came. I saw a long rising stretch of grass to the south. Shivering violently, I went cautiously back to the sea. The apparently steep cliff resolved itself into a very easy climb, for the boat had crashed into a comparatively shelving, rocky bay.

Slowly I trudged up the turf, and as I did so I came more and more out of shelter into a driving wind. The storm was still blowing, still blowing out of the southwest.

With the strengthening light the explanation of the night's events became obvious— I could see the cliffs rearing high into low clouds, three or four miles away to the northeast. They were the cliffs of the island of Great Blasket. O'Dwyer had been more delayed by the wind and sea than he realized and had started me, not south of Dingle at all, but a full ten miles farther to seaward. And I was now on the low flat island of Inishvickillane. It was clear why I.C.E. had discontinued the lighthouse on the Tearaght. Had it been working we should never have made this mistake.

Feeling that somewhere I had heard of a similar situation, I began to explore the island. It was maybe three-quarters of an hour—but it seemed longer—when at last I found a quite substantial house. I walked toward it, gloomily realizing that although I had got myself successfully beyond the barrier, my position was completely hopeless. Then I remembered that in Stevenson's *Kidnapped* David Balfour had simply been able to walk off Earraid when the tide went down. But there would be no walking off Inishvickillane. My boat was a wreck, and I must give myself up, right at the beginning. I was "run-out" without receiving a single ball.

11

THE CLIFFS OF INISHTOOSKERT

It was pointless to struggle further, cold, wet and hungry. I might as well give myself up immediately, I thought, as I walked up the winding path to the stone house. Whoever lived there wasn't going to enjoy being wakened at this early hour, but this was clearly the occasion to be hanged for the sheep rather than the lamb.

In response to my hullabaloo, the door was opened by a sleepy-eyed, middle-aged fellow in a dressing gown. I suppose I had expected to find a local small farmer, tending a flock of sheep with a little fishing as a side line, and the story I had prepared was designed for the consumption of such a person. It was accordingly very disturbing to hear an American voice say: "Where the hell are you from?"

"Oh, I'm more or less an ordinary devil washed up by the sea."

"Well, in that case come inside. But how did you get here?"

"From the sea, as I've just said."

"But for God's sake, you don't mean you were shipwrecked on a night like this?"

"There's no other way I'd be standing here. Our boat went down."

"How many of you are there, for heaven's sake?"

"Two others drowned in the sea, I'm thinking."

My manner must have been suitably grave, for in truth I was seriously worried about Mike and Slugeamus. The great

124

thing was that they could always stand in behind Brandon Head. This would give shelter from the southwest, so that the odds would be in their favor.

"Well, we must look for 'em without delay."

"And what would I have been doing this hour past but looking for me friends?"

The man left me for a moment to return with a dressing gown. "Take this robe. The bathroom is the second door to the right. When you're through, come into this passage. It leads straight to the kitchen."

With muttered thanks I did just as he advised. It was a terrific relief to get off my salt-drenched clothes. I had to run the water quite cool at first to avoid smarting. At length, feeling very tired but very much better, I returned to the kitchen, wrapped in the dressing gown and carrying my dripping things. There was the smell of frying bacon.

"I've got an air search started. There's no reason to give up hope yet."

This was a nuisance, for I had no wish for Mike to be spotted. Several things were clear. From the excellent fitments in the bathroom and kitchen this was no farmhouse. Rather was it a farmhouse converted into a luxury residence. Plainly I had stumbled on a comparatively influential person, as I could judge from his last remark. Equally plainly, my story would sound painfully thin, but I was sufficiently exhausted to be past caring.

As I ate ravenously, the fellow looked me over curiously. "I'm baffled to understand how you came to be at sea," he said. "Where are you from?"

"Kilkee."

This shook him, as I expected it would. "But that's fifty miles outside the area! How did you ever get yourself as much lost as this? Boy, you're in the wrong ball park!"

"Poaching."

"I'm sorry, I don't get it."

"The best sole on the coast is to be found in Dingle Bay. When the weather's bad, but not too bad, we're often after coming down here to get what we can. It doesn't pay really, but it's a sport with all us fishermen outside the barrier."

"You weren't expecting this storm, I suppose."

"No, sir. The reports were of a choppy sea and a strong breeze, but no storm."

"All this is news to me."

I had no doubt at all of this. It was a preposterous story, but my presence there at least gave it some slight substance. If this amiable fellow didn't like it he was welcome to think up a better one for himself. The true explanation looked preposterous too.

My host produced a pair of pajamas and showed me to a bedroom as soon as I had finished breakfast. It was now about 6:30 A.M. I tumbled into bed and fell asleep.

It was dark when I awoke. With the light switched on, I found that clothes—not my own—had been put in the room while I slept, and also a razor, soap and toothbrush. By the time I was ready to go downstairs I looked reasonably respectable, pretty well for the first time in the last two months, in fact since I left Dublin.

Perhaps I should explain that there seemed to be six or more bedrooms upstairs, but that downstairs, apart from the kitchen and the bathroom I had used in the morning, there was just one single very large room.

I made my way to the latter room, and was very surprised to find six people there. There was the American of the morning; two girls and a man of curiously mixed coloring, dark skin, light hair; a third girl, a good-looking, genuine blonde; and a third man, apparently of about thirty.

There were no introductions. The third man said, "So this is your fellow from the sea, eh, Homer?" Then he turned to me with tones of command. "You may go into the kitchen and cook whatever you fancy."

"Thank you, sir."

I left for the kitchen feeling well pleased in spite of this abrupt and contemptuous dismissal. The genuine blonde followed me.

"I'd better show you where the things are to be found," she said.

It was a little embarrassing to display a hearty appetite when my companions were supposed to be entombed in a watery grave. Worse, the blonde began to ask questions about how I came to separate from the two of them and about the final landing on the island. I took the line of answering in monosyllables and blew my nose vigorously. Eventually the girl left, so that at last I was able to settle down to a really good meal.

There were indications that the storm was blowing itself out, which was all to the good. Mike and Slugeamus would surely be away toward home, even if they had been obliged to stand to during the day. I washed up the dishes in good heart, for I had received a slice of the most tremendous good fortune. Even by the light of early morning the American had looked familiar. He was of course Homer Hertzbrun, the Nobel Prize-winning nuclear physicist. More important still, the third man, the man who had ordered me peremptorily to the kitchen, was none other than Arthur Mitchell F.R.S., the chemist from Cambridge. This was the man that I had been told to watch for particularly, one of the very first scientists to join I.C.E. and a possible key to the whole business.

This being the case, I had no intention of remaining immersed in the domestic quarters. Whatever it might require in the way of cheek or brass, I was determined to get back there into the lounge. Turf burns quickly and is soon used up, especially on a stormy night. A new load is always welcome to any company. So I looked around until I found the supply dump and a large basket. Then with a full load of the stuff I opened the lounge door and walked in with the best confidence I could muster.

Two other men had evidently joined the gang. Probably they had been outside, walking the island, when I had first appeared. I closed the door quietly on the inside and began unloading the turf. Soon I was quite forgotten, however, for a tremendous argument seemed to be going on. I sat unmoving by the side of the fire, listening.

At first I could make out little of what was going on. The argument was clearly very one-sided, however. There seemed to be five against one, with two sitting out. The genuine blonde and one of the new men were the sitters-out. The solitary fighter was one of the half-blonde girls.

The five were very sure of themselves. The solitary girl was equally sure. Whatever abstruse physical (or mathematical?) question was under discussion, she gave all the indications

127

of knowing exactly what she was talking about. She had an odd appearance; a jolly-looking face, but a face that decidedly wasn't jolly. This jolly-girl-that-wasn't began to get very exasperated, as one might do in talking to a crowd of exceedingly dull, obstinate people. The five, with the confidence of the majority, kept firing all manner of objections at her.

The scene was fast becoming very acrimonious when the mental fog in which I had been immersed suddenly cleared away. I saw where the trouble lay. Perhaps I had better explain.

In two dimensions a circle divides the plane into two parts, the "inside" of the circle and the "outside," both parts being simple connected. All this is obvious enough. The same result is true for any closed curve in two dimensions that can be put into a continuous one-to-one correspondence with a circle. So far so good.

Now the majority of five were generalizing this theorem to higher dimensions in the course of their argument, and I knew this to be already wrong in three dimensions. Without pausing to heed the consequences, in the bright clarity of the moment of perception, I said so.

The half-blonde girl nodded a curt approval. "It's nice to find somebody with a little elementary common sense," said she.

"What do you know about it?" snapped Mitchell.

"In science and mathematics it doesn't matter who speaks, only what is said," I answered.

"I did not expect a fisherman as an ally," said the girl.

Then I saw the enormity of what I had done. But I was a mathematician first and an agent a long way second, and this I had no wish to alter.

Even as they moved to attack, I saw that my one hope of deception lay in keeping within a hair's breadth of the truth.

"Let's get this right. You did say you were a fisherman, didn't you?" asked Hertzbrun.

"Of course I did."

"And is it common these days for young fishermen to be well informed on the finer points of topology?"

"Look here, sir, you wouldn't expect me to blab out on

your doorstep the whole story of my life. I had to make some sort of selection, and the relevant selection was that I happened to be a shipwrecked fisherman. Remember that I expected to find a shepherd or a fisherman here and not a scientist; it seemed pointless to explain that I was a student temporarily employed as a fisherman over the summer."

"And where would you be a student from?"

"Cambridge."

"See here Mr.—?"

"Sherwood, Thomas Sherwood."

There was a slight silence. Then Mitchell went on, "See here, Mr. Sherwood, as a fisherman there are two very queer things about you: one that you're shipwrecked in forbidden territory, and the other that you seem to be a singularly well-informed mathematical student from Cambridge. What I want to be clear about is the connection between these peculiarities. I imagine you're not going to pretend that there is no such connection?"

"Of course not. There's the perfectly obvious connection that any self-respecting undergraduate would do his damnedest to get into a place like this. As soon as you forbid him to do something he'll do it for sure, just for devilment."

"That explains the psychology but not how it was done," said the half-blond man, with the same slightly peculiar accent as the mathematically minded girl. It had rather the sound of someone who speaks Gaelic as a first language.

"Did you get permission to visit the west coast?" asked Hertzbrun.

"Naturally not. I got permission to visit Dublin and various points to the east. But I worked my way over to the west, not taking the various rules and regulations very seriously, I'm afraid. When I found that fishermen outside the area were in the habit of poaching down this coast, just as I said this morning, I decided to join the ranks. There's quite a shortage of men you know, so I'd no difficulty in landing a job. My idea was to get as near as possible to what you're pleased to call 'forbidden territory.' Sooner or later I felt there'd be a chance to get in."

"And are we asked to believe that you just happened to be wrecked by chance and your companions drowned?"

"Of course not. I soon saw that the right way to get in would be with a small motorboat. I persuaded the skipper of my trawler to let me make a shot with an old boat that I managed to put together. Unfortunately we were seriously out of position, due to the gale, when I started—far too much to sea down the bay. I expected to land near Dingle instead of here. And indeed I feel very badly about this miscalculation, since it has led me into abusing your hospitality, I'm afraid."

"You can repay us by giving details of this trawler that carried you so close into our coast."

"You must know that I can't do that. For consistency with what I said this morning, let me only say that there were three of us and that we were out from Kilkee."

I felt this to be well managed. They wouldn't believe my last glib statement, and that was Mike's best insurance. Kilkee would be the last place where they would look for the errant trawler. The inquisition ended with a sarcastic laugh from the "jolly-girl-that-wasn't." The other half-blonde girl turned to her also with a laugh.

"Fanny, this looks like quite a chance, doesn't it?" But what the chance was I couldn't guess.

As often happens after a summer storm, the next day was bright and clear. When I came down to breakfast, the genuine blonde was alone in the kitchen.

"They're having a business meeting today," she said. "I'm not in on it, so I thought we might go off in the boat, if you haven't finished with boats for good and all."

It was a nuisance to hear that I couldn't spend the day with the whole party, for I knew in my bones that I was now within a stone's throw of the solution to the whole problem. Still, if they were having a meeting I could hardly barge in, and there would always be the evening anyway.

"And where have you a mind to go?" I asked.

"There's some quite nice scrambling on one of the islands. I see by your boots that you're a mountaineer. How about going over for an hour or two? The rock is surprisingly good."

We packed lunch and set off. The boat was a far more powerful affair than the one I had wrecked. It forged easily through the still heavy sea, driving from wave to wave, the sun sparkling all around us.

"This is where one of the galleons of the Armada came through," shouted the girl as we made the passage between Blasket and the mainland. The Tearaght appeared to the west, and the cliffs of Inishtooskert lay ahead.

I was now feeling as well as it was possible to feel. After the weeks of walking, and after the lifting and hauling of nets, I was exceedingly fit. The world around me was ablaze with color and light, and I had an exceedingly pretty girl to spend the day with.

We found an anchorage on the south side of Inishtooskert.

"Go ahead," I said. "I'll just check the mooring ropes again."

The girl led the way, almost at water level, until the cliffs steepened above our heads. Then she unslung a nylon rope.

"Let's start with this. It's quite easy really."

We tied on and the girl took the lead, climbing very easily up the first pitch of thirty feet or so. I had made three trips with the Cambridge Mountaineering Club, and, although I am no expert climber, it was without misgiving that I followed behind. The climb was no more than "moderate," and in any case I had the moral support of the rope.

At first I had made no attempt to "lead," because evidently the girl knew the climb. But soon I realized she was a couple of grades better than I was. As we moved up the cliff I had the exhilarating experience of following an expert on a climb that was within my capacity. It was possible to imitate her light, delicate, almost dancing movement. Under these conditions one invariably climbs at one's best, indeed often beyond one's real ability.

We made three separate ascents of the whole cliff, all by different routes. Then at the island's summit we sat down to lunch. This was a day of color. The mainland was aflame— the bog, the stubble fields, the avenues of rowan trees, the line of Eagle Mountain. The sea was deep blue, except where it shone and sparkled like a vast jewel.

After lunch, the girl said, "Just one more climb, and then I think we ought to start back. They should have finished their meeting by the time we return. What d'you say?"

I said that I thought one more climb was a fine idea. In truth I was feeling in excellent shape.

The new route lay farther to the east, near the "fin" of the island. After a tolerable first twenty feet, it became difficult. But behind such a leader I had no worries. We struck the first "severe" pitch about a third of the way up. This was beyond my real capacity and by rights I should have protested and returned. But what young man would make such a protest to a very beautiful girl who climbed with such effortless grace? I would be all right with the rope as safeguard! She took the pitch like a Greek goddess heading for Olympus.

The next pitch, a long one without any adequate stance, was no better. It started from a good foothold, going at about sixty degrees up a long smooth slab. The holds were very small, no more than little knobs in the rock. Even the start was exceedingly awkward, a step up from the foothold onto a slight excrescence situated almost at shoulder height. Had this come at the beginning I would have pocketed my pride and said no very firmly. But now it would almost be as bad to return as to continue. I got up somehow. A pitch no more than "very difficult" followed. I used far too much brute strength on it.

By now we were some two hundred feet up, not too far from the top, thank goodness. But there was still trouble left, a shockingly steep climb over a projecting nose, with holds that were just adequate. I was panting pretty hard as I came up over this nose onto a wide stance. The girl was taking in the rope, a smile on her face.

"Jolly good," she said. "That's the last bad bit. I know it's pretty awkward the first time. There's just the boulder now."

We were in a not-too-steep gully, jammed by a huge boulder. At first sight there seemed no way over this last obstacle. It was true that the boulder projected out of the gully on one side and that tolerable holds could be seen far out on that side, but they could not be reached.

"How on earth does this thing go?"

"Impossible for one, easy for two. A perfect argument against solitary climbing" was the answer.

"You give me a shoulder, so that I can reach the top and

haul myself up. Then I secure the rope from above so that you can swing out onto those good holds over there."

And of course by this combined tactic it was perfectly straightforward, if not "easy." It was certainly a far simpler matter than the pitches we had just come up. So I gave her a shoulder, and with something of a struggle she managed to heave herself over the rounded top of the boulder. "Harder for her than for me," I thought, as I looked at my holds four yards away to the left. They looked rather good.

"I'm up," she shouted, as she started to take in the rope. She kept taking in slack until the rope tightened between us.

"That's too much. Give me about three yards," I shouted back. The rope slithered on the rock, and I saw an end come down, not the usual end, but an end that had been neatly cut. Equally neatly, I had been limed and snared.

I was now alone with an unclimbable boulder above and an almost unclimbable cliff below. And with devilish forethought the girl had left me with only twelve feet of useless rope. I shouted furiously, but there was no reply. I heard the faint sound of boots on rock, and that was all.

I find it difficult, even months afterward, to write of this situation without my feet sweating. The route up the cliff must have been chosen with appalling cunning. My first move, if I was to descend, lay over the steep nose, and this is the one sort of pitch that it is genuinely more difficult to descend than to ascend. The trouble with descent is to find holds for the feet, since they cannot readily be seen. When the rock is steep and the holds are small, one is only too likely to be left scrabbling vainly with the feet, hanging by the fingers—for a little while.

This I realized as I looked stupidly at the severed rope. What I did not realize was that all the clues were now in my hand, all the clues necessary for solving the mystery of I.C.E. Yet I wasn't to arrive at the solution for nigh onto another year, perhaps because I was to be led away from the main issue by clues apparently more patent, but in fact misleading.

Right now, however, I was congealed on the cliff, unable to move up or down. And as I stood immovable and irresolute,

I became acutely aware of the boom of the sea striking the base of the cliff 250 feet immediately beneath my feet. I tried not to look down, but my eyes seemed ever drawn to the blue water. I watched it heave and burst into masses of foam.

I expected to become crag-fast, a state of paralysis in which the climber loses all sense of balance. He clings desperately to the rock until exhaustion comes and at last he falls to his death. Instead I became furiously angry. Suddenly I had a desperate desire to catch up with this hellcat of a blonde. I would knock all Hades out of the girl once I caught up with her.

It would help to descend in stocking feet, for then my toes could feel the indentations in the rock. I managed to get my boots off, but one of them slipped. It hit the cliff face once on its journey to the sea, disappearing with a slight splash. My morale must have been greatly improved by the flaming rage that consumed me, for deliberately I also dispatched the fellow to a watery grave. The faithful boots in which I had walked through Ireland were gone, and with them a chapter closed.

Although I was now almost anxious to begin the descent, there was one thing more to be done. I have a good photographic memory. I forced myself to review all the holds by which I had climbed. I made a mental map of each of the separate pitches. Then at last I started downward.

The bulge was terribly difficult. I forced myself to take the weight on my toes. I would explore downward with one foot, find at last some indentation and then gradually transfer the weight to the lower foot. The climbing was very slow; the danger and temptation was to make too much use of the hands. Even at a distance in time of nearly a year, as I write these words I notice little beads of perspiration on my thumbs.

The "very difficult" pitch seemed easier than on the ascent, and no wonder after the steep bulge I had just come down. Then I reached the top of the great slab. But now it was less difficult to see the holds, and I had two advantages that I didn't have in the ascent. My stockinged feet were more sensitive to the nicks and knobs in the rock, and the friction of any clothing on the rock provided a useful upward force. The last step down the slab onto the ample foothold below proved exceedingly awkward, however. I was trembling very markedly when I reached the foothold, the trembling coming from muscles that had been taut and strained for too long.

But now I knew that I would get down. There were still two shortish severe pitches before I reached the lower easy rocks. I took the pitches without undue haste, but I went down the lower rocks very quickly.

"Now my girl, you can look out for yourself," I thought, as I felt in my inner coat pocket. My fingers closed on the distributor cap of the motorboat engine. I had removed it before we started off in the morning, when I was pretending to look to the mooring ropes; for as I have said before, I am of a suspicious mind. The girl had cleverly taken me in, I must admit, but now the score was even. She couldn't start the boat, and my turn was to come very shortly.

12

THE INDUSTRIAL CORPORATION OF EIRE

And so in a fine old temper I scrambled rapidly along the rocks that bordered the sea, in haste to get back to the anchorage. But I was still a way off when I heard a familiar roar, a damned helicopter again. Somehow the genuine blonde must have got word across that she was marooned on the island. Obviously they had come to pick her up.

I raced up the slope, trying to reach the top of the island before the girl could be taken off. But human muscles compete poorly with the internal combustion engine, and I was still some way from the summit when the helicopter rose again and moved away over the sea. I had to be content with the futile and ineffective gesture of shaking my fist at the wretched thing as it passed almost overhead.

There was no point on this occasion in trying to conceal myself, since my safe descent of the cliff would be obvious as soon as the boat put out from the island; *if* the boat put out, that is to say, for there was just the possibility that the girl might have put the engine completely out of operation. There seemed little reason why she should have done so, but I was apprehensive as I made my way downhill to the mooring spot.

"How easy is a bush supposed a bear!" My fears were groundless; nothing in the boat had been touched except that a small W/T set had been taken from its container. This was how the girl had managed to bring help so quickly. I had been foolish not to have noticed this little piece of radio equipment.

It took but five minutes to replace the distributor cap, turn on the petrol and start the engine. Although I was in a tearing hurry to get back to Inishvickillane, I made a detour to the end of the island to a point where I could see the horrible climb on the cliff. From a quarter of a mile out to sea it seemed impossible that even a fly could have come down it. With a shiver I realized something that had not occurred to me before—this part of the cliff was indented in such a way that it could not be seen from the mainland. If I had stayed stuck to the rock I wouldn't have been seen, and there would have been no real hope of rescue.

The boat pitched and rolled quite considerably as I drove her at full speed into the waves. It was rather like taking a car rapidly along a road covered in potholes. But I cared nothing for the boat, only so long as it got me back safely to the island. What I wanted right now was an interview with Dr. Mitchell and his friends. I was too mad at the time to appreciate the methods of I.C.E. If the girl had got me to swing out to the boulder, *and then cut the rope while I was swinging,* nothing could have saved me. But that would have been murder direct, and apparently they drew the line at this. A fine sense of delicacy persuaded them to put me in a position where I would kill myself, where I had only myself to blame, a position from which I ought to be able to extricate myself—for it is a cardinal rule of rock climbing that nobody should ascend a crag unless he is competent to descend it.

Why had they decided to get rid of me? How had I given myself away? My impression was that I had told my story reasonably well. It was possible, and even likely, that they would still be suspicious of me, but there is a great margin between suspicion and certainty. And surely only people who were absolutely certain would commit murder? Attempted murder it had been morally, however one might play on words.

Then I saw where my mistake lay, glaringly obvious. When I had stripped off in the bathroom the previous morning and taken my wet things to the kitchen I had unwittingly handed over my trousers without removing Colquhoun's money. And the money had given me away. No student would carry anything like so much. I cursed myself for a wet fool.

Now I was a mad fool. I drove the boat, slapping and racketing along the same course that the galleon of the Armada had traveled four hundred years ago, and then I turned to the southwest, heading directly toward Inish-vickillane. The boat ran more smoothly as I came into waters that were sheltered from the southwest wind. I brought her in quickly to the landing place, made fast and started up the path to the house.

In a powerful rage I opened the door without knocking. There was nobody in the kitchen, nobody in the sitting room, nobody upstairs. It was plain that the birds had flown, probably taken off by helicopter or some such device. I went back to the kitchen and found my trousers still hanging before the fireplace. A quick inspection showed the money to be still there, but I did not draw the correct inference. By now I was shunted onto a logical sidetrack.

I had just decided that my trousers, the ones hanging there, were distinctly inferior to the ones I was now wearing, and I had just transferred the money, when I was startled by a voice behind me. "Mr. Sherwood, I believe."

I swung around to find a small oldish fellow, to my jaundiced eye a little weasel of a fellow, standing in the doorway leading to the lounge. The adrenalin was still flowing strongly, so that my instinct was to pick him up and shake him soundly. I took a couple of steps forward, and then, only then, noticed the dark silhouettes of three massive men standing beyond the weasel. The four of them stepped into the kitchen and I saw that the weasel's companions were in uniform. These were members of the I.C.E. police. The flow of adrenalin stopped, and discretion dominated.

"Yes, Mr. Sherwood? Shall we talk in here, or would you prefer the lounge?"

"There is little to be gained by disturbing ourselves," I said taking a seat.

"Very well, then. Now I think we ought to have a quiet talk. Let me introduce myself. The name is Earnshaw, Howard Earnshaw."

This was superfluous, for Howard Earnshaw, sometime professor of metallurgy in the University of London, was another of the people that I had been warned to look out for. "A wild man, a fanatic," Parsonage had roared at me.

"My name is apparently already known to you," I remarked.

"Your name, and your career. If I may say so you have the beginnings of a very fine career."

I bowed, and this ratcatcher of a fellow went on. "But why, oh why, Mr. Sherwood, must you go about things in such an odd and roundabout way? Why not come straight to the front door if you are interested in I.C.E., and I gather by your presence here that you are. We are not in the habit of turning promising young men away empty-handed; just the reverse."

"Well you see, there's the possibility that I might stay on at Cambridge and take a Ph.D. But I thought it wouldn't do any harm to have a look round before making up my mind."

"And didn't it occur to you that there might be some objection to your 'taking a look around'? Suppose every prospective candidate for a job at I.C.E. were to decide to snoop around as you've been doing. Don't you think that would be rather unpleasant for us?"

"I'm afraid it just didn't occur to me to look at it in that way."

"Well now, Mr. Sherwood, I'm going to speak quite frankly. Normally we deal very severely with people who deliberately make an illegal entry into Kerry. But I'm the first to admit this would be somewhat absurd in your case. To be shut away would do you no good, and it would do us no good either. So what I'm going to do is to treat your case exactly as if you'd made an application for a post directly from Cambridge."

Somehow I managed to avoid any show of surprise. During the last few minutes it had gradually dawned on me that Mr. Weasel could know nothing at all about the business on the cliffs of Inishtooskert. But what did it all mean? Who in their senses would first try to kill a man, and then, when the attempt failed, would immediately turn round and offer him a job? The correct explanation actually occurred to me, but I dismissed it without much thought. I had become hopelessly confused, which was what the real authorities of I.C.E. wanted.

Aloud I said, "That seems a very fair offer in the circumstances, sir. But I think I ought to warn you that I'm rather an individual sort of worker."

Plainly I was now back to winning small points again.

"I think you'll find that I.C.E. has sufficient elasticity to provide the right sort of working conditions for even more curious people than yourself, Mr. Sherwood."

"You said that you'd treat my case as if I'd applied for a job in the normal fashion. Can you tell me what this means?"

"It means that you'll be entitled to the normal salary scale: for entrants with a good university degree, fifteen hundred Irish pounds per annum. That'll be your case. Subsequent salary increases will be largely a matter for yourself. If you are good to the corporation, the corporation will be good to you."

"That seems a very decent proposition."

"I wonder if you realize what sort of organization it is that you'll be joining, Mr. Sherwood?"

"To be frank, sir, it's just because I can't answer this very question that I hesitated about joining the corporation."

Earnshaw sat back and grinned in the manner of a death's head, no doubt imagining that he was unbending in a pleasant style. "Many people seem to think that there lies a mystery where in fact there's no mystery at all. I.C.E. is *science*, science in control of itself, an organization run by scientists. In the world at large science is forced to serve many masters; here scientists are asked to serve only science itself. This is the real explanation of why we are forging far ahead, of why in a few short years we shall have none to rival us."

"That makes everything a good deal clearer."

"I am glad of it. Let me put things more crudely in terms of money. The great nations of the world value science so poorly that less than one-tenth of one per cent of their productivity is spent on basic scientific research. In contrast we spend approximately twenty per cent. In fact we are now spending more in total on basic research than all the nations of the world. This may seem an astonishing statement but it is true nevertheless, for the expenditure of the rest of the world is only a little more than one hundred million pounds per annum—a trifling sum, my dear fellow."

I said that it all sounded like a great opportunity for a young man to have.

"A very great opportunity. There is no telling how far an able young man like yourself may be able to rise."

In this at least the man was prophetic. Had he been able to foresee the course of events I think he would have expired instantly.

"Well now," he purred, "this is all very satisfactory. I have a few papers here which I'll sign for you. Then you can take off straightaway for Headquarters."

He handed me the papers. "Now let's hope you'll have no more trouble, Mr. Sherwood."

Two of the policemen led me outside and onto the beautiful grassy plateau of the island. As if to maintain the theme, a helicopter was waiting.

There was still the possibility, admittedly remote, that some "accident" was to be staged.

We took off and gained height over the bay. Everywhere along the coast was a line of foam, a reminder of the passing storm. The islands were similarly girdled as they lay in blue water. There were high clouds, streaked by upper winds that were still strong, and the bright purple color of the mainland seemed even more intense than I had remarked earlier in the day.

But it wasn't to this scene of wild beauty that my attention was mainly directed. An aerial trip provided a unique opportunity for getting an idea of the layout of the I.C.E. industrial plants, as they ranged over the flat boglands around Cahersiveen. Now I could see them clearly on our right, so vast and extensive as to suggest interesting notions. It was very easy to pick them out because of the great roads with which the whole system was linked.

But it was the new city of Caragh that really took the eye, built in the beautiful valley some five miles to the south of the lake from which it takes its name. Instead of the grays and dull browns of the average city seen from the air, Caragh is ablaze with color. Instead of standing apart from the surrounding countryside through its drabness, it is distinguished by its brilliance. This is achieved largely by the cultivated flowers which occupy much of the total area of the city. The buildings themselves are chiefly noticeable from the air for the flashes of reflected sunlight, mainly a golden effect achieved by some translucent dispersive material.

The buildings become immediately more dominant as soon as one lands, their colors more alight. Caragh is not a vast, unwieldy collection of small hutches, like the other cities of the world. It contains but sixty-odd buildings laid out in great avenues, no more than seven or eight to any particular avenue. Taking advantage of the natural slope of the land, and of the ample water supply, small rivers run past the buildings. At night, the whole city is lit by a soft diffuse light.

Let me dispose now of my own petty affairs. On landing I was directed to a place which seemed to be a species of high-grade recruiting office. I was given a temporary room in what I suppose might be described as an hotel, and was handed a preliminary cash advance of twenty pounds Irish, not that I had any real need of the latter. I bought various necessaries and a volume of Shakespeare's *Comedies*. Then I sought out the best restaurant in the city and treated myself to a wonderful meal, by way of celebrating an entry into a new life.

After dinner I spent a couple of hours walking entranced

through the city. At last I was where I wanted to be—I was "in."

Now I must deal with a question that might possibly trouble a reader of this report. Wouldn't it have been vastly more simple to have reached Caragh by the straightforward method of applying for a job with I.C.E.? Why go to all this fantastic trouble?

There were three reasons for the apparently indirect, roundabout approach that I had actually adopted, each a strong one. It is not in my nature to be actively deceitful. I simply couldn't have set myself to work against an employer who had accepted my services in good faith. I would, moreover, have reached Caragh without any real confidence in myself, a solitary individual pitted against an enormously powerful organization.

This was of course the situation now. But curiously I felt no misgivings. The successful descent of the cliffs of Inishtooskert seemed to have given me an enormous confidence. Moreover, this latter affair had left me fighting mad, and this was perhaps the most important of the three reasons I mentioned above. If I had not been in a deep cold rage I would soon have been seduced by this beautiful city. I would soon have taken off my coat and worked in earnest for I.C.E.

At length I returned to my room. Before turning in I read a couple of acts of *Twelfth Night*. This gives a picture of the apex of society as it was four centuries ago, I thought. There are many things that we can't do nowadays: we can't write like Shakespeare. But of a certainty no earlier generation than ours could have built such a city as Caragh. The society of four centuries ago would have thought themselves on another planet if by some magic they could have been transported here. Indeed to people of our own age it almost looks like authentic science fiction. But Caragh is something strange but real, for it is the city of the third millenium, the city of the future.

13

SOME INFERENCES

In my conceit I imagined that the logical taproot of I.C.E. would soon be exposed. Now that I had reached the nerve center of this great enterprise, I even began to think about ways and means of getting out of Kerry once I had accumulated the necessary information. I little suspected that I was embarking on the most baffling section of the whole affair.

Luckily, during the first months at Caragh I started to work quite genuinely. For some time I'd wanted to learn about modern field theories in physics, and as the winter progressed I became more and more engrossed in this subject. So I was able to preserve some degree of sanity as difficulties began to pile up all around me.

But I did make odd scraps of progress. One day I had occasion to refer to a paper in the *Astrophysical Journal*. In flicking through the volume in question, I noticed a place where a couple of exclamation marks had been inserted in the margin. I was too bound up in the thoughts of the moment to pay much attention to this minor detail. A few days later, however, when I needed to look up the same paper in order to settle a remaining small point, I remembered the exclamation marks and decided to see what they were about. But the marks in the margin were nowhere to be found.

Feeling still only mildly curious, I then looked for traces of rubbing out, but I couldn't find any. I have a good memory, as I think I've mentioned before, and there was no doubt in my mind, within a page or two, where the deface-ment had occurred. The surface of the paper in the margins was entirely smooth, in a way it couldn't possibly have been if a rubber had been used, even very lightly. This was an entirely different copy of the volume but in a similar binding. Why?

Naturally I read through the investigation that happened to be situated at the place where I believed the marks to have been inserted. It dealt with the problem of electrical pinches in the solar atmosphere. The general idea was that the solar atmosphere is pervaded by tubes of magnetic force, rooted below the photosphere. These tubes become twisted through the motion of the dense material at their roots, but this twisting doesn't in itself produce any serious instability. If for instance a tube becomes so seriously twisted that contraction sets in at any place, the very action of the pinch itself increases the pitch of the helix, and so restores stability.

The main notion was to let two such tubes come together at a particular place. Then if the fields penetrate each other at the point of contact, a violent contraction must occur when the helices are so wound that the longitudinal components cancel and the circular components of the magnetic field augment. In this case, a region of instability is held firmly out from the solar surface by the strength of the stable supporting arms of the tubes, which act as the filaments of an arc.

In a flash I remembered the "corpus" floating in the sea—what was it? Twin helices, senses opposite! This might well be the clue to the thermonuclear reactor. Here was a way in which a high temperature region could be held away from the boundary of a vessel, on magnetic springs.

It was obvious what had happened. Some informed person had noticed this paper, containing quite unawares the germ of the right idea. Unable to restrain himself he had added the exclamation marks.

Another point was equally obvious. My movements must be under very close surveillance. Even so, this business with the *Astrophysical Journal* had been rather clumsily managed. I reinserted the exclamation marks and returned the volume to the shelves.

I think perhaps that I ought to give some outline of my ideas about the real nature of I.C.E. as I had them at this early stage. In certain respects the general picture didn't turn out to be too far wrong, although the most essential step was still completely beyond my comprehension. Here then is the position as I saw it.

Starting with straightforward matters, it appeared that I.C.E. employed about half a million persons, working and living for the most part on the south side of Dingle Bay. I was curious at first to understand how this large population was housed without its being necessary to construct at least one tolerably large city.

I suppose that in ordinary homes each person has a space allowance of roughly 100 cubic yards. A large building, say with a volume of 200,000 cubic yards, suitably shaped to be divided into apartments, would house about 2,000 persons. It followed that the whole population could be fitted into about 250 such buildings, which together would cover an area of only some 400 acres. Since I suppose the area of land available must be some 30,000 acres, it was clear that an impression of enormous spaciousness could be achieved—each building could be surrounded by more than 100 acres of garden, woodland and seashore.

In my opinion a lot of nonsense is talked about lack of privacy under such conditions. There is one overriding prerequisite; complete soundproofing. Provided this is satisfied there is no reason why one shouldn't feel just as private, just as remote from one's neighbors, in an apartment as in a detached house. I had learned this when I lived for three years in College at Cambridge.

The often-heard argument that apartments are unsuitable for families with children is of course correct if the apartment block is set in a city, surrounded by busy streets. But the argument is scarcely true for an apartment block set in woods and fields, with a nearby stream.

So I had to reckon on half a million well-paid, well-satisfied employees of I.C.E.

This number of people may seem large at first sight. Yet it

was plainly out of proportion—in the sense of being small—compared to the industrial activities of I.C.E. This could mean only that enormous use must be made of automation.

Now let me say something of the scale of this industry. By now I could see clearly the difference between I.C.E. and the older established industries of Europe and America. The latter grew up around specialized mineral deposits—coal, oil, metallic ores. Without these deposits the older style of industrialization was completely impossible. On the political and economic fronts, the world became divided into "haves" and "have-nots," depending whereabouts on the earth's surface these specialized deposits happened to be situated.

Britain ran ahead, first of Spain, then of France, because Britain was more of a "have" than her rivals. America ran ahead of Britain because she was still more of a "have." Russia based its rise to dominance not so much on the invention of new techniques as on the deployment of hitherto unused resources. Sweden was a "have," Austria was a "have-not." All this was industrialization of an early primitive kind.

In the second phase of industrialism, the industrialism now apparently perfected by I.C.E., no specialized deposits are needed at all. The key to this second phase lies in the possession of an effectively unlimited source of energy. Everything here depends on the thermonuclear reactor, the clue to which had fallen so recently into my hands. With a thermonuclear reactor, a single ton of ordinary water can be made to yield as much energy as several hundred tons of coal—and there is no shortage of water in the sea. Indeed, the use of coal and oil as a prime mover in industry becomes utterly inefficient and archaic.

With unlimited energy the need for high-grade metallic ores disappears. Low-grade ones can be smelted—and there is an ample supply of such ores to be found everywhere. Carbon can be taken from inorganic compounds, nitrogen from the air, a whole vast range of chemicals from sea water.

So I arrived at the rich concept of this second phase of industrialization, a phase in which nothing is needed but the commonest materials—water, air and fairly common rocks. This was a phase that can be practiced by anybody, by any nation, provided one condition is met: provided one knows exactly what to do. This second phase was clearly enormously more effective and powerful than the first.

Of course this concept wasn't original. It must have been at least thirty years old. It was the second concept that I was more interested in. The concept of information as an entity in itself, the concept of information as a violently explosive social force. Put two or three hundred engineers, chemists, back in old Roman times and let them be given a chance to show what they could do! Within a decade or two they would have turned Roman civilization topsy-turvy and made a mockery of the apparently important issues of the time.

It was here that I came to the big problem. How came it that I.C.E. possessed this great block of new information, while the older industrial nations did not?

There was one solid argument in favor of the Earnshaw point of view. It was certainly true that the major industrial nations were spending only tiny proportions of their national incomes on acquiring the new block of information—on basic research, that is to say. In the case of the United States for instance, the amount spent was only one-thirtieth of one per cent. Earnshaw had been dead right about this.

Why should a nation drag its feet in such a way? Why should it refuse to press on toward the rich rewards that the second phase of industrialization would give? I believed I knew the answers to these questions.

Our ordinary ideas about social and economic stability depend upon new knowledge not being injected into society at too rapid a rate. Could it be that older industrialized nations, when faced by a choice between scientific advance and preserving a social *status quo,* all preferred the latter alternative? If so, this was certainly a big point in favor of Dr. Weasel's opinion.

Even so, I couldn't believe it to be the explanation I was looking for. Scientific advance at a maximum rate would cause one nation to forge slowly ahead of a less progressive nation. The gap between the two would widen gradually decade by decade; the gap would eventually become very great, but only after a generation or so. There would be none of the explosive advance of I.C.E. This could come only from a massive, sudden injection of a large volume of new information. From where? This was the rock on which I foundered whenever I tried to think the matter through to a conclusion.

14

CAGED

Naturally I would dearly have loved to get back into the northern peninsula of Kerry. But this peninsula, together with the part of the southernmost peninsula west of Adrigole, was absolutely out of bounds, not only to me but to everyone else with whom I came in contact. This entirely confirmed my suspicion that much of what I wanted to know must lie with Mitchell and his friends. Try as I would, however, I simply could not pick up the track of these people.

It was a great temptation to try my former raiding methods. I thought of attemping to force a route through the mountains to the north of Dingle. I thought of taking a boat down the Kenmare River and of sailing around Valentia Island and thence across Dingle Bay. I even thought of stealing a helicopter. But a moment's thought showed all these ideas to be mere wildcat schemes. Such methods had proved exceedingly difficult even when I was outside I.C.E. territory, even when I was unknown to the I.C.E. security police. Now that I was obviously under close watch—as the incident of the *Astrophysical Journal* plainly showed—it would be outright nonsense to try any more cloak-and-dagger stuff. The moment had come for sheer logical reasoning.

As far as material considerations were concerned, I had no

cause for complaint. I had a very pleasant apartment in Caragh. I was able to get a quiet cottage in Ballinskelligs Bay, to which I often went down at week ends.

I made many acquaintances but no real friends during the three months before Christmas. It was quite staggering to find everyone wholly incurious about the underlying organization of I.C.E. The general disposition was to follow the statements expressed to me by Earnshaw. Beyond this, nobody seemed to care. Why be curious when one is onto a good thing? Why dissect a goose that is laying eggs of gold?

Or was there a more sinister explanation? It seemed rather unnatural that none of the young fellows of about my own age seemed in the least bit worried about the logical problem that was plaguing the life out of me, the problem of what was really at the bottom of this I.C.E. Moreover, it was quite clear that nobody was being allowed to talk with me too much. I would strike up a short friendship with someone—we might spend a couple of week ends together, perhaps in the mountains or by the sea—then invariably the man would be shifted to some other job, or he simply wouldn't turn up for an appointment. This happened time and time again, and, although I was angry at first, I eventually came to accept the situation. I had done all I could to reach Caragh, and it was obviously no good fussing now that I was there.

I remembered the remarks of the true canon, the ones about the I.C.E. medical service. Was it possible that all these people around me had been conditioned in some way? I looked carefully at the work of my young colleagues. Was it more competent than original? Frankly, I was too inexperienced to be sure, but more than experienced enough to be suspicious. At all events I was glad that my health was good. I resolved to give nobody the opportunity of shooting any drugs into me.

My one weak spot was food, not eating too much, but that I had to eat at all. I was at pains to think of a plan that would make it exceedingly difficult for anyone to tamper with my food. I made a rigid rule that I would take all my food and drink from large-scale self-help restaurants. I never took any dish that wasn't on display and that wasn't reasonably popular, for it was most improbable that a large number of people would be dosed with some noxious stuff just to get hold of me. And I made the situation much more complicated by varying the places where I ate and the timing of my meals in a random fashion— I got some slight amusement by using the non-recurring decimal representation of π to make my choices, two digits for each meal.

There was one exception to the disruption of incipient friendships: a young fellow called Womersley persistently kept inviting me out to dinner. Although I had no hesitation in refusing him, I managed for a time to make reasonably polite excuses. When, however, in the face of this discouragement he still kept on, I decided at last to avoid further embarrassment by putting the matter to a test. This really was a mistake, even though I managed to win the first round without difficulty.

I met Womersley, a tall pale fellow of about twenty-eight, one evening in early December. We drove in his car to a restaurant about three miles outside Caragh. As I expected, hors d'oeuvres, salmon and cold meat dishes were on display, so it was not at all awkward to get past the first courses of the dinner with reasonable safety. The sweet and the coffee would be altogether another question, however.

Womersley droned on about the merits of the wild duck he was eating. I answered by saying that the only dish I would have preferred to the salmon would have been curried mutton. The point was lost on him, however, since he was obviously no student of the great Sherlock Holmes. Before choosing my salmon I had left Womersley for a moment to make a telephone call to the Caragh Information Office. I asked the office to call me back in half an hour with some tolerably complicated information about vacant cottages in St. Finan's Bay, and I gave Womersley as my name.

My companion ordered chocolate ice cream and coffee, and I did exactly the same, hoping that my timing would be reasonably accurate. I was lucky. I kept Womersley talking for a couple of minutes after the waiter had brought the order. This was sufficient. The man came back with the news that Dr. Womersley was wanted on the telephone. I interchanged the ice creams and coffee.

Womersley was bound to be suspicious, if he wasn't the

simpleton he pretended to be. I might possibly have been spotted changing the sweets, although I did this pretty quickly and our table was fairly well out of view in a corner. These considerations didn't trouble me very seriously, however, for Womersley must now eat the sweet unless he wanted to make an issue of it. And somehow I didn't think he would dare to make a fuss. My impression is that he was under orders to be discreet in public at all costs. Anyway, he ate the ice cream and drank the coffee—not quite all the coffee, I noticed.

I insisted that we return to my apartment, since I preferred drinking my own brandy to risking Womersley's. We started a game of chess, probably the strangest I have ever played, both of us expecting the other fellow to fall sick. I studied Womersley's face carefully as he made his moves, and he for his part stared at me as I made mine, which I did quickly.

The transition was amazing. One minute the man was studying the board, the next he was staring at me, his face contorted with an odd mixture of anger and apprehension.

"You tricky bastard," he yelled. "You'll get yourself fixed good and proper for this."

Then he jumped up and made for the door, but I seized him by an arm and spun him quickly into a chair. I noticed little drops of perspiration on his forehead. He tried to get up but I pushed him back.

"I must get to hospital. Don't you understand?"

"I understand all right. You'll get to hospital in good time. But first I want to know who put you up to this business."

"I don't know."

"Stop playing the fool. Who was it?"

"I don't know. I tell you I don't know," he moaned.

The drug was taking effect at an alarming rate. I suppose it would have served the man right if I had kept right on bullying him, but his distress was now so obvious that I simply couldn't bring myself to persecute him any longer. I rang the hospital and told the Duty Officer that Thomas Sherwood was sick.

It took very little time indeed before a doctor arrived, a man I would say in his late thirties, to my eye not a very pleasant fellow. He marched into my apartment, asking, "Where is he?" in what I took to be an unctuous tone.

"You had better go downstairs," he added. "There will be an ambulance in a minute or two. You can show the men where to come."

Without going out of the apartment, I slammed the outer door. Then I tiptoed back to the living room. The doctor was injecting something into the wretched Womersley. The faint groans died away, and I heard the man say, "Well, well, Mr. Sherwood, quiet at last! Now we shall see what we shall see."

Then I saw red. I took hold of the fellow and slammed him really hard against a wall.

"May I introduce myself? My name is Thomas Sherwood."

"But . . . I thought," he stuttered.

"You thought that this silly fellow here was Thomas Sherwood. You know you medical people are so full of your drugs and needles that you seem to have no idea of how unpleasant a physicist could be if he were so minded. I might get you to eat a little boron, for instance."

This took him by surprise. "But boron isn't . . ."

"Boron isn't a serious poison in small quantities? It would be after exposure to a moderate flux of neutrons, my nasty little man. I'd take you where the neutrons wouldn't hurt me very much, but where they'd cook the insides out of you." Then I grabbed him again and slapped him hard with my open hand.

Was I getting as bad as the wretched Tiny? No, I think not. This whole affair smacked of concentration camps and secret police. But something really had to happen now. I.C.E. Security simply could not take this incident lying down. Besides the cards were on the table, and discretion was no longer of much importance.

Just as once before in Marrowbone Lane, I made my plans in a flash. I was out of the apartment in an instant. The ambulance attendants were still in the road outside the building. I told them to go up to Apartment 619. My first intention was to drive away in the ambulance, in some respects an ideal vehicle to escape with. But then I realized that Womersley might be really ill; it might be important to get him to hospital quickly. The drug had certainly acted with an astonishing swiftness, perhaps indicating a serious overdose. I decided to get away by bus to Killarney and thence on foot.

This might appear a wholly precipitate change of plan, but I had long ago made up my mind about the terms on which I was prepared to carry on the fight against I.C.E. I was willing to do what I could single-handed against this powerful organization. I was willing to be jailed; I was even willing to take a severe physical beating, but I was not willing to risk any change in my personality. I am an unrepentant sinner. I would prefer to go to hell as I am, rather than go to heaven as I am not.

It would be the best part of an hour before the bus left, so I dropped into a fairly crowded café. I would then be far less likely to be picked up than if I spent the hour standing around at the bus station. I was shown to a table where a man was eating a sandwich and drinking coffee. I wasn't hungry, but for the sake of appearance I also ordered coffee and a sandwich.

The best plan seemed to be to cross the frontier at the place I knew so well in the Boggeragh Mountains. The whole nature of the frontier defenses made it much easier to get out than to get in. I thought that if I could get as far as Killarney I would have a sporting chance.

Suddenly I realized that the man at my table was studying my face rather intently.

"I wouldn't try it," said he.

"You wouldn't try what?"

"I wouldn't try making a getaway on one of the buses, on the one to Killarney for instance."

Then he laughed in my face. "You haven't got a chance, my boy. I followed you right from Building J." Superfluously, he went on. "As soon as I saw where you were heading, I slipped in here ahead of you, and told the waitress to show you to my table. Very simple, eh?"

"Commendably so. If you need any recommendation for promotion I shall be happy to act as a referee."

"Shall we be going, or would you like to drink your coffee first? I need hardly say that it would be quite pointless to make any attempt to escape. We have you surrounded, and the roads can be blocked at a moment's notice."

Ah well, back we go to winning small points again, I thought to myself. Aloud I said, "I think I'll finish the coffee, if you don't mind?"

"Oh, not in the least."

With bowed shoulders, and a slow gait, I went ahead of the man. But as soon as we were out of the door I whirled on him, as I had once whirled on the wretched Tiny. But this was a vastly easier proposition. The first punch was beautifully placed. He went down soundlessly like a fairground dummy. In an instant I was away down the road, heading toward the center of the city. There was more than a chance that the fellow was bluffing and that I was not surrounded at all, at any rate not for the moment. There had scarcely been time for one man to get on my track, let alone a whole squad.

I had gone about two hundred yards when two cars came toward me. They passed by, heading for the café. I cursed myself for a fool in wasting time over the coffee. Plainly my only hope now lay in an outrageously wildcat scheme. There was a helicopter landing square very close, and I headed at full speed toward it, hoping that I might find a machine in readiness for take-off. I had no idea at all about flying one of the brutes, but this was obviously the moment to learn.

I now had a fantastic run of luck. I was nearing the place when I heard one of the wretched things coming in to land. With complete assurance I walked to the square. I managed to get in without any challenge. I saw two passengers alight. The pilot got out on some errand or other, and without the slightest hesitation I walked toward the machine. Still without any challenge, I fumbled with the catch on the door. It seemed to be very stiff and far more difficult than it should have been. At last there was a clear space in front of me, and I was hauling myself into the cabin. But now I knew only too well that something was wrong, badly wrong. The coffee that I had insisted on drinking had been drugged. I slumped down into the pilot's seat. My last thought was to try to will myself to bridge the gap of unconsciousness that I knew was to follow.

I had just one vision, of bright lights, of voices, and a startlingly clear impression of the half-blond man whom I had seen on the island of Inishvickillane. Then I found myself awake and perfectly well, back in my own bed in Apartment 619, Building J.

I knew it to be a Sunday, so I shaved, took a shower and dressed in leisurely style. It was a little surprising to find no Sunday papers to read over breakfast. I was also a little surprised to find that although I was thirsty I seemed to have little appetite for food. I packed a picnic lunch thinking to go for a three- or four-hour walk. Plainly I was in need of a blow in the fresh air.

It was only when I reached the road outside Building J that the situation became clear. This was not a Sunday. Everything was wrong; the sky was too dark, the air too chilly, and there were no flowers. This was more like a day in December than one in early October. I bought a news-paper and found that indeed the date was December 9, 1970. For some reason, there was a gap of more than two months in my memory. My last clear recollection was of arriving from Dublin by air in early October.

Although I was somewhat mystified by the situation, I wasn't seriously worried. I had planned to go for a walk, so off I went. I caught sight of the sun at about two o'clock, and from its low position in the sky it was manifest that the December date was correct.

When I returned to my apartment I made a search through my papers to see if there was anything to throw light on the missing months. I found letters from I.C.E. addressed to Trinity College in which the terms of my appointment were clearly stated. Sure enough, there was a copy of my own letter saying that I would arrive by air on October 2, just as I remembered it. There was the stub of my airline ticket from London.

The problem was cleared up by a doctor, a jovial old boy who came to see me in the evening.

"Ah it's nice to see you back in the land of the living," said he.

"And why shouldn't I be in the land of the living?"

"My boy, you've had a really bad blow on the head. Lucky you've got a skull made of steel."

"Where did it happen?"

"You've forgotten?"

"A whole two months seem to have dissolved away."

"Ah well, that's scarcely surprising. Temporary amnesia is very common in such cases, although I'm a bit surprised that it extends over as much as two months. The thing to do is to keep absolutely quiet for the next few weeks. Perhaps a little gentle walking, but don't go out too much. I'll make arrangements for food to be sent up here to you. And there are various sedatives that you ought to be taking twice a day. Try to get some sleep after lunch. It gives any ruptured blood vessels in the head a chance to heal."

"But what in heaven's name was the trouble?"

He lifted a finger and wagged it in a fatherly manner. "You aren't the first young fellow that I've had to caution. Avoid fast cars, my boy. The next time you may not be so fortunate."

This explanation took quite a weight off my mind, and feeling distinctly sleepy I went to bed about nine o'clock.

Once again I turned the matter over in my head when I awoke the following morning. I was glad to find my memories of the previous day perfectly clear and sharp, so that plainly my brain wasn't impaired except by the loss of two months, which after all wasn't a very serious matter.

Instead of taking a shower, I filled the bath. Lying in the water I suddenly noticed the marks of hypodermic needles in my thighs. Idly I wondered why one should be given injections for the treatment of a blow on the head. Perhaps there had been lacerations too. I looked myself over but couldn't find any. There were no bruises either. Odd! Except for my head, which surely must be badly bruised. I felt slowly and gingerly. No pain anywhere, which was even more distinctly odd. I increased the pressure and still no pain. I certainly must have a skull of steel, just as the old fellow had said. Thoughtfully I shaved.

After breakfast, I looked again through the file of letters, those that I had written and those that I had received from I.C.E. Two more odd things. One of the I.C.E. letters mentioned physics and I had done no physics in my Tripos. And as long ago as May I had made arrangements to change my rooms in Trinity from Bishop's Hostel to Great Court. Yet my letters were addressed in August and September from Bishop's Hostel.

It seems incredible that I sat for an hour trying to reconcile all these facts before the first seeds of real suspicion entered my head. When they came, they came with a rush, however. Suddenly I knew with certainty that there had been no motor accident. I knew with compelling certainty that the missing months had been crammed tight with crucial incident. And with these certainties there came the suspicion that the letters in my file must be false, and that I might not have arrived in Caragh City from Dublin by air on the second of October. How I had arrived I could not say, for my mind had not only blankness in it, but many things that were false. Yet I had won my first victory. My curiosity was aflame.

The old doctor came to see me once again, bringing exactly the same advice as before, together with more medicines. Instead of accepting them, I went to the bathroom to fetch the first consignment of whatever stuff it was that he was trying to persuade me to swallow. I handed it back to him, saying that perhaps he would have better use for the material than I had. He smiled in a rather kindly way as if to say "good luck," bowed and left the apartment without further comment.

For the only time in my life I came near mental breakdown in the days that followed, for try as I would I could gain no entry to my missing memories. I was convinced that they were tucked somewhere in my brain, but nothing I could do seemed to wake them into consciousness. It was like the frustration of trying to remember a forgotten name, but a thousand times worse.

I had papers in my files relating to the cottage in Ballinskelligs Bay, and on the third week end after my awakening I decided to go down there. Friday was fine, so instead of using the bus, I walked along the hills overlooking the mouth of the Kenmare River. From the upper slopes of Mullaghbeg I lay on a rocky ledge watching the ever-changing swell of the sea breaking endlessly over richly colored rocks. My fingers touched a rough boulder and in an instant the memory of the appalling descent of the crags of Inishtooskert became alive again. Like the island itself, this solitary memory reared up sharp and clear out of a sea of oblivion.

A fine day is often followed by wind and storm. So it was on that particular week end. At the height of the gale I put on oilskins and made my way down to the edge of a roaring sea. Foolishly I went too close to the water and was hit by the flying top of a great wave. Even as the spray was driving furiously into my face I knew that another chord had been set in vibration. I knew that I had arrived in Kerry by sea, and in just such a storm as this.

After supper I built a great turf fire. Over a pot of coffee I worked away to extend the two breaches I had now made into the world of black uncertainty. Slugeamus was my next victory, and with him came Mike O'Dwyer and then Colquhoun. There was no longer any frustration. Methodically, like a jigsaw puzzle, I fitted the whole picture together. I worked both backward and forward, rediscovering detail after detail. Occasionally whole blocks of experience would suddenly click back into place. It was four in the morning when I retired to bed, exhausted but triumphant.

My memories continued to sharpen in the days that followed, until with the passage of a week the whole story had become every bit as clear as it had ever been. But I knew that I was only half victorious. I knew that in some subtle respect, one that I could put no name to, I had been changed. Something was different in me, and my agitation of mind was not decreased by a sense of mysterious uncertainty. I am the first to admit that I was appallingly slow in finding the solution to the major mystery of I.C.E., but I feel no shame in my failure to deduce the nature of the change that was even now taking place within me. At all events it was not a change that reduced my determination in the least degree.

15

CHANCE PAYS A VISIT

As January passed to February, I came more and more to feel how completely I had been isolated. "Birds of a feather . . ." Unfortunately there were no birds of my particular feather anywhere to be found in Caragh City. My only appreciable conversations were with the farmers I might meet in a day's tramp among the hills, or with fishermen in Ballinskelligs Bay at week ends.

One afternoon, however, I happened to be in a store when I caught sight of a familiar head.

"Well, by the saints if it isn't Thomas Sherwood!" exclaimed Cathleen. "Bull, me husband, often speaks of you," she added.

"Bull?"

"Me name's Bradley now."

Then I remembered Bull Bradley, an experimental physicist from my Cambridge days. He was so named, not from his sexual proclivities, but from the roars with which he used to lead the forward line of the Clare College Rugby fifteen. He was just the fellow to have tackled the monster back at Slievenamuck, and to have gotten his head broken for his pains.

Cathleen invited me to dinner at their apartment, where Bull Bradley greeted me with great heartiness.

"Sherwood, old boy, nice to see you."

Then he roared with laughter. "You remember that manuscript of Cathy's you threw away? Well, it wasn't any good, you know. A deliberate piece of nonsense. We turn 'em out by the dozen in our department." This remark persuaded me to keep the conversation at a purely social level.

The evening passed pleasantly and at the end I naturally returned the invitation. But although the return was accepted, it never in fact came to pass. Cathleen rang me up one afternoon asking if she could see me for a few moments.

When we met later, she said, "Thomas, I'm wondering about coming out with you on Thursday. I'm wondering for Bull's sake, you see."

"There's been some talk about me in Bull's department?" She nodded. "They suspect you very much, Thomas. You must be careful."

As we parted for the third time, she put her hand on my arm. "It's sorry I am about those papers."

Colquhoun had been very confident about Cathleen. Was it possible that this partnership with Bull Bradley had more to it than met the eye? In any case my acquaintance could only be an embarrassment to them, so it was clearly right that I should keep myself out of their way.

In fact this was my last attempt at any form of social life. I saw that I must accept the position of Ishmael, my hand against everyone. After all, this is what I had asked for and this is what I had got for my pains. As the months rolled on I was to become bitterly lonely, but at least there was one profit to be rung from the situation: I was able to work at a furious pace. Otherwise it would have been only too easy to have succumbed to the unaccustomed luxury in which I was now living.

The weather was rarely good these days, but very occasionally the week end would be clear and fine and not too cold. Then I would walk to my cottage by the sea.

A singular affair arose out of one of these trips to Ballinskelligs Bay. I should perhaps explain that my cottage is set aside by itself in a rather lonely spot. It had often occurred to me that if I.C.E. really wished to dispose of me nothing could be easier—but then the blonde girl might have settled the matter back on the cliffs of Inishtooskert simply by cutting the rope at the right moment. In some curious way I had a belief that an intellectual battle was really being fought—that the authorities in I.C.E., whoever they might be, preferred to use psychological rather than physical weapons.

One Saturday evening at about eleven o'clock there came a knock at my door. A man fell across the threshold as soon as I opened up. His head was heavily bandaged, his clothes torn, and he seemed to be suffering from multiple flesh wounds, not too serious as far as I could judge. But his left knee joint was giving him so much pain that he had been obliged to crawl a considerable way to the cottage.

The poor fellow revived somewhat after he had lowered a large tot of whiskey.

"Would your name be Thomas Sherwood?" he asked in a Devon accent that warmed my heart.

"Yes, it would."

"D'you have any identification?"

"Letters, books, a passport. But I might have all these even if I wasn't Thomas Sherwood."

"Which is true enough. But you answer the description, all right. I haven't much time, so I'll have to take the risk."

"You seem to have taken plenty already. Before taking any more, perhaps you'd better explain why you've come here."

"Because I happen to have the same boss."

"Meaning who?"

"During winter storms the waves beat heavily on the western strands."

"This is the right moment to buy vegetables on the London market."

"Or fish for that matter, if you have a taste for it."

"I see. And how did you know that I was down here at this cottage?"

"Sherwood, you're a suspicious devil, I must say!"

"It's just that I like to get the picture clear."

"I believe you have some acquaintance with Cathleen O'Rourke—a Mrs. Bull Bradley she calls herself now. Anything more?"

"I see what you're driving at, Mr.—?"

"Chance, John Chance."

"Very well, Mr. Chance, what d'you want with me?"

"If you look outside you'll find a rucksack. Better take a flashlight."

I found the rucksack. It was stout and very heavy. I carried it into the cottage.

"That's exactly what I want you to do."

"I don't understand."

"I want you to carry the rucksack for me, nothing more, about seven miles to the St. Finan's Bay road. There'll be a car waiting when you get there."

I poured him another whiskey. "Suppose you tell me a bit more. What's in the sack?" Instead of replying, he took large swigs at the whiskey. I unfastened the top of the rucksack and managed to slip my hand down the side.

"Wireless equipment, eh? I thought as much from the weight."

"You haven't learned much discretion, have you?"

"Not very much, I'm afraid. But unless I learn a lot more about you and about this rucksack. Mr. Chance, I'm certainly not going to carry it a single yard."

"Still not satisfied with my credentials, eh?"

"Perfectly. I simply want to know what game you're playing."

"And suppose you get yourself caught?" said Chance. "Don't you think it might be better for you not to know what game I'm playing?"

"Maybe so. But it's not my way of doing things."

"All right then, Tom, you've asked for it. I suppose you can guess that I got in here by parachute. Crocked my knee, damn it."

"Where did you land?"

"Toward the top of Coomakista Pass. I had the devil of a job getting as far as this."

"But why go carrying a sack of radio equipment around the countryside?"

"That's our alarm clock. It must be got to St. Finan's Bay before dawn."

"You mean it's a trigger?"

"It's a hell of a trigger, Tom lad."

His face twisted with a spasm of pain. "Some more whiskey, please. This damned leg is giving me merry hell."

"Where's the bomb?"

"Near Castletown, of course. That's where I.C.E. has all its defense precautions. Once they're blown sky-high, we can simply send our chaps in at leisure."

"I can see that. What I don't see is why a wireless transmitter had to be dropped by parachute. If our men have been able to assemble a bomb, surely they could manage a transmitter."

"Ever tried to smuggle anything out of the Castletown area?"

"Couldn't a time device have been used?"

"I imagine it was considered, but that wasn't thought to be the best way. I'm not the general, you know. I'm just a chap in the trenches who does what he's told."

"But why take all these risks? Why not trigger the bomb from the air?"

"To make certain of the coding. That's why this thing has simply got to be hoofed to St. Finan's Bay. They have the final code setting there, brought across by boat."

It was just the sort of muddle-headed situation that fitted my own experience. But it had a horrible chance of succeeding. I picked up the rucksack.

"Where exactly is this car? I'm going to be darned tired by the time I reach it."

I trudged slowly along the road. Each time a car came past I slipped off the rucksack, putting it down out of sight at the roadside; then I continued walking without it. Once the car was past I returned to pick it up again. The main danger was in getting through Waterville. Here I simply had to risk being seen. It was a spine-tingling ten minutes before I was safely on the far side of the little town.

By now I could appreciate Chance's point. There were situations in which it was not wise to know too much. Tens of thousands of people were going to be killed. The problem of I.C.E. was going to be solved, not intellectually, but by battering it out of existence. And suddenly I knew it was not going to happen. There was soft bog to both sides of the road. In a few minutes I had moved a hundred yards to the left. I slipped off the heavy load, ripped out half a dozen metal boxes and sank them one by one into the squelchy ground. Returning to the road, I walked another mile before abandoning the rucksack itself.

I was too hopelessly miserable to turn for home, too hopelessly miserable to do anything but impale myself on the guns of the desperate men who were waiting in the car a couple of miles ahead.

The St. Finan's junction appeared at last. The dark shape of the car was just visible against the light-colored road. I walked quickly toward it. There was nobody inside. I turned just in time to see a dark figure rise from the roadside. A light flashed in my eyes. I was on the point of hurling myself forward when a vaguely familiar voice rang out. "And what might you be doing here, sir?"

The light went off. I flicked on my own flashlight and saw a guard from Waterville with whom I had a passing acquaintance.

"Oh, Mr. McSweeney, I didn't recognize you. I'm on a late tramp and getting pretty tired too. I saw the car as I passed the junction and wondered if by any chance I could get myself a lift along the road."

McSweeney was joined by a second guard, who asked, "And who might this be?"

"It's Mr. Sherwood. He lives on the other side of Waterville."

"This is a late hour to be on the road, but—"

"That's true too. I'll be glad when I can climb into my bed," I replied.

"Would you have seen anybody walking the road?"

"I was passed by an odd cyclist, and by several cars."

"Which way have you come?"

"Over the Ballaghasheen from Caragh."

"A powerful distance."

"That's what my feet are saying."

"Would any of the cyclists have been carrying a great rucksack?"

"Not that I could see."

"Well, well, it can't do any real harm if we take Mr. Sherwood home. Get into the car, Mr. Sherwood."

I was relieved to find both guards climbing into the front seats. I might be under suspicion, but I was not yet under arrest. More alarming, what if these were John Chance's confederates, the men I was supposed to be meeting? Plainly I must prevent the guards from entering the cottage at all costs. I could deal with Chance, but I could scarcely hope to deal with three desperate and angry men.

I got out of the car at the entrance to the little lane that ran down to the cottage. The guards got out too.

"We'll see you down the lane, Mr. Sherwood. Just to make sure that everything's in order," said McSweeney.

"That's very kind of you, but I shall be perfectly all right. I'm only tired; not crippled, you know."

"Some pretty queer customers are abroad tonight, and not the little people either," said the other guard with a chuckle.

"We'd like to see you home, Mr. Sherwood, as much for our satisfaction as for yours," added McSweeney.

So I had no choice but to lead the way. Thank heavens the cottage was in darkness. I opened the door—it was actually unlocked, but I rattled my key to make it sound as if I were unfastening the place. I switched on the light, thanking my lucky stars that I had been tidy enough to wash up after supper. The whiskey bottle and Chance's empty glass lay on the table. I grabbed two clean glasses.

"Have a snifter before you go," I remarked, slapping out the spirits in generous quantity before they had time to reply, for I was scared they would smell the stuff.

"Well, it isn't an Irishman's habit to refuse."

I noticed they darted glances about the place as they drank. But it wasn't easy to tell that I had already arrived at the cottage from Caragh during the late afternoon—if Chance kept quiet everything might still be saved.

"Thanks for the sensation, Mr. Sherwood. We'll be going our way, now that you seem to be all right here."

They stepped outside and I accompanied them, ostensibly to offer further thanks for the ride. They moved off toward the lane. I returned to the cottage, but I waited with the door open, listening to their progress down the lane. I heard the car start up and drive away, but of course only one of them might have gone and the other might be returning, so I locked the door and drew the curtains. I put a kettle on the stove, which would be the normal thing to do after a long tramp. The temptation to run upstairs or to shout was almost irresistible, but I realized that Chance might not have drawn the curtains and that an injudicious use of light might easily make him visible from the outside.

I waited as long as I could—perhaps half an hour—until the tension became unbearable. Then I took the bull by the horns. I switched on an upstairs light, going quickly from the one bedroom to the other. Chance had gone. I am half ashamed to say that I looked under the beds and in the wardrobe, but Chance had vanished, game leg and all. I am not a solitary drinker, but on that occasion I poured the last of the whiskey into a tumbler and tossed it down in a couple of gulps.

I fell asleep after lying for about an hour, turning and twisting the incredible events of the night, trying to fit them into a pattern that had at least some semblance of rationality. It was just graying dawn outside when I was wakened by the loud ring of the telephone. In some apprehension, I went down the steep cottage stairs as quickly as I could. A girl's voice asked if it was Mr. Sherwood speaking. When I answered that it was, she simply laughed and immediately rang off.

By now I was quite hungry, so gloomily I cooked breakfast, thinking that from the moment I left Cambridge I seemed to have been surrounded by a raving pack of lunatics. If I could have viewed the happenings of the last eight hours without preconceptions I think I could have made sense of them. But the only line of reasoning that seemed to hold the slightest consistency led to such an apparently monstrous contradiction that I was not bold enough to follow it to an end.

The thing that worried me most about this strange affair was a strong feeling that this wasn't the first time I had seen Mr. John Chance. But where and when I first met him I could not think. My memory might still be playing an odd trick, of course.

16

BREAKTHROUGH AT LAST

I am going to pass over several months' happenings rather quickly, not because this was a fallow period—I do not remember ever having worked so hard—but because most of my work was of only personal relevance.

Among the scientific activities that I discovered, two might be very briefly mentioned. I saw many more "moving mountains," of the sort I had first glimpsed in Dublin. These machines, of the size of small ships, were of course nuclear-powered. They were used for earth-moving operations. The almost incredible speed with which new buildings were erected and the surrounding landscape changed owed itself in a large measure to these giant monsters.

A great deal was apparently going on in the biological field. One point about which it was easy to get information deserves special mention: the extermination of flies and insect pests in general. There may be some who will regret the passing of the mosquito and the midge, but I am not to be numbered among them.

In my attempt to catch up with Mitchell and his friends one of the obvious dodges I tried was attending the main weekly scientific seminar at Caragh. There was no security involved, so I'd no trouble in gaining entry. But even though these meetings were well attended by the higher grades of scientific personnel, Mitchell and Company never appeared.

This was the beginning of an important train of events,

however: events that started in a small way. I was anxious to cause all the disturbance and disruption I possibly could. Outright defiance of restrictions seemed foolish and unprofitable, since the odds were obviously too much against me. But there was no harm in trying to inculcate a sense of inferiority in the scientific personnel, and I thought I saw how to do this.

I noticed a curiously contradictory feature of these weekly scientific meetings. Anyone who could ask intelligent questions of the lecturer of the day gained great prestige. And if the lecturer made an error that one could correct, then better still. In spite of the reputation that could be won in this fashion, nobody took the trouble to prepare himself in advance—apart from the lecturer, of course. Nor was it at all difficult to prepare oneself, because the subjects of the meetings were always announced at least a week beforehand.

So in addition to my own work I deliberately began to read up carefully in advance on all manner of topics. Sometimes the subjects were fairly mathematical. These were not only the easiest for me to cope with, but they were also the greatest prestige winners. I had more trouble with experimental physics and with chemical and biological topics. Yet a day or two's reading was usually sufficient to suggest several questions. The great thing was that nine out of ten of the audience would be following the lecturer only rather vaguely. Then if one could ask some precisely formulated question, the effect of a complete understanding was created.

I took up a position in the middle of the second row, leaving the front row for men of established reputation. It was astonishing how quickly the system took effect. Within a month the high and mighty were looking at me with averted vision. Within two months they were nodding openly. Within three months I had a recognized seat in the front row.

This policy had two effects. The more immediate, and the less important from a long-term point of view, was that I was asked to give a seminar myself, i.e. to be the lecturer on a certain day, the subject to be of my own choosing. Now it was indeed lucky that I had been hard at work during the past five months, for I did have something new to talk about, not completely developed it is true, but interesting. I chose as a topic "The Interpretation of Electric Charge as a Rotation."

One day I had a conversation with one of the older scientists. Would I undertake the solution of a set of equations that had proved very puzzling? They were of a non-linear partial type that could only be tackled numerically on a high-speed digital computer. I agreed to this proposal because I particularly wanted to gain some experience in the use of such a computer.

The special difficulty of the equations was that derivatives with respect to each of the variables became so large in certain ranges of the variables that it seemed impossible to store a lattice with the usual property of small changes of the functions from one lattice point to the next.

Once I had agreed to tackle the problem, I set about it with great energy, if only to prevent my new-found reputation from sagging too badly. The first step, and the most difficult, was to decide the mathematical method of attack. Then came the job of coding for the computer, which was of the ultrahigh speed, superconducting variety. Naturally I started by building up a stock of sub-routines. These I tested separately until they were working properly. Then came the big job of fitting all the individual pieces together and of writing the logical program for controlling their operation.

It was well past high summer before everything was working properly. I was now ready for producing results. This meant that instead of needing the computer for a few minutes at a time I would be requiring long "production" runs, each lasting an hour or more. Clearly I should soon find out whether I.C.E. was really serious about this problem, or whether the idea was merely to keep me busy and quiet. In the latter case, they would soon jib at providing adequate time for these long runs on the machine.

As things turned out I had no serious complaint to make. I got a fairly adequate ration of time on the computer, not as much as I'd have liked, but then nobody ever gets as much time as he would like. Since the program worked pretty well I was soon on good terms with the machine manager and with his staff. I had an arrangement whereby I'd take over the computer whenever it happened to be free. This was fairly often, because plans for machine operation made in advance frequently go awry. So it was with many who were officially scheduled to use the machine. Things would go wrong, the instrument would lie unused, and then I could step in. By this device I was able to extend very considerably the amount of time for which I was able to operate the computer.

I mention all this to explain why I got into the habit of examining the machine schedules pretty closely. It annoyed me considerably that no shifts were normally worked over the week ends. The waste of the computer seemed scandalous, if not downright wicked. But I was told that there simply wasn't enough work to justify the extra staff that would be necessary for week-end operation. I suppose this was right, for with a computer of such great speed the amount of calculation that could be done in a five-day week was quite fantastically large. Still, it seemed a shocking waste.

On Monday, Tuesday and Thursday the computer was run from 9 A.M. to 6 P.M., and from 8 P.M. to 7 A.M. The intervening short periods—viz. 6 P.M. to 8 P.M., and 7 A.M. to 9 A.M.—were used for engineering maintenance. On Wednesdays and Fridays the computer was run from 9 A.M. to 4:30 P.M., and there was no night shift. Naturally I was curious about this difference, and my curiosity was sharply augmented by my complete failure to find any explanation for it. When I mentioned the matter to the machine manager, he jumped so violently that I was very careful to say nothing more.

The obvious tactic was to try to get a run that would last right up to 4:30 P.M. on one of these latter days. It was a long time before success came my way, and then only as a result of a double accident. The manager was on holiday, and his assistant's wife was expecting a baby. One Friday, the assistant phoned to say that the computer was available from 3 P.M. to 4:15 P.M., but that on no account must I continue to work after 4:15 P.M. Foolishly he told me that he himself would not be in the laboratory that particular afternoon. This meant that I had only the young operator to deal with, and I knew he would be anxious to get away for the week end, probably with his wife to the sea.

It was something of a dubious trick to assure the young fellow that he could leave at 4 P.M. I made all the necessary motions to indicate that I was "packing up" and told him to go off, saying that I would set a new roll of paper in the "printer" as soon as I had all my tables, cards and tapes collected together. By now I had learned how to operate the machine pretty well, and I had worked with this particular operator fairly often. So, being Irish—and therefore no instinctive stickler for rules and regulations—he left me to my own devices at about 4:05.

I restarted the computer with a scarcely ruffled conscience. When 4:15 came, I continued to let the machine calculate. Slowly the minutes slipped away. I was on tenterhooks lest someone should come in. The following quarter of an hour provided the first case of a lack of security that I could recall since my entry into the services of I.C.E. Someone should certainly have been detailed to make sure that the computer had been vacated. It is strange indeed how easily a simple security precaution can be overlooked at the end of a week in the holiday season, especially on a really beautiful day.

The clock came to 4:30 and still there was no interruption. The computer went merrily along, chattering out its results. Then I was aware that someone had come in very quietly. I was examining the results at the printer, and I forced myself to go on doing so for maybe half a minute.

"Oh, I'd no idea the machine was in use."

"No, you can have it straightaway," I replied.

"If there's something you want to finish . . ."

"No, no, I can output the calculation onto tape and pick it up later."

I flicked a switch, and one of the magnetic units came immediately into motion.

"All right, I'm finished now."

I moved over to retrieve the tape with my unfinished calculation on it, intensely conscious that I had just managed to win a round in this long-drawn-out game. For the intruder was none other than Fanny, the half-blonde girl who had been right about her topology when the other five were wrong, back so long ago on the island of Inishvickillane.

I watched out of the corner of my eye as her deck of cards went into the "reader." Plainly it was a very big program, some three times the size of my own. Since the difficulty of a program depends about on the square of the number of instructions, this had roughly ten times the difficulty of mine. Pray heaven it doesn't work, I thought uncharitably—otherwise I'll be getting the inferiority, not I.C.E.!

The machine worked for perhaps ten seconds and stopped. The girl, swearing *sotto voce* to herself, keyed in a manual instruction and immediately a group of numbers was hammered out on the printer. Then the girl retired to study her program together with the numbers. Time crept on. Five o'clock came and I was in an agony lest someone in authority should find me there. I was sorely tempted to seek some redress for the day on the cliffs of Inishtooskert, which I had by no means forgotten. But I kept quiet at a distance while she worked away. I think the computer must have been lying idle for some forty-five minutes before she got up with a long sheet of new instructions that had now to be inserted manually into the machine. In this way it was possible to modify the program at an enormous expense of operating time.

"You'd better read out the instructions, and where you want 'em to go, while I do the keying," I said.

We worked for about half an hour, flicking the keys. I concentrated really hard, determined not to make an error, which is only too easily done. Then we cross-checked all the changes, reading from the machine as it was now modified against the girl's list. When at length she was satisfied, one more instruction was keyed—to start the computer calculating again. "It can't possibly work," I said to myself, "not after all this agony." But it did. At least it didn't stop this time.

The girl sat over the printer, watching the numbers that were tapped out from time to time. She compared them with a handwritten table taken from a file.

"It looks to be working all right now—as far as I can tell.

"Well, well, I must say for a fisherman you seem enormously versatile," she added.

"I'm afraid my program is a very modest affair compared with this," I said, indicating the machine and its present calculation.

"What are you doing?"

I gave a brief sketch of my own problem.

"You know," she said, "I had an idea you were around Caragh when I saw a notice of a seminar on the nature of electric charge. Perhaps you could tell me about it over dinner? I want to get about another hour's work done. You don't mind waiting?"

In the circumstances waiting was the last thing I minded.

When the machine had been switched off, and we'd gathered together our respective belongings, I asked the girl where we should go. With the first grin I'd seen from her, she answered. "One of the public places."

We packed our things in the back of a car parked close by the lab. While the girl drove, I guided her to a good restaurant about five miles to the south, one that wouldn't be too noisy. Our entry was marked by some curious glances from one or two of the tables.

I took this to be a tribute to the girl's appearance, which in truth was very remarkable—violet eyes, light hair and a skin that looked as if it had been deeply tanned by a month of climbing on sunlit snow mountains. She appeared to be in her early twenties, but I had a suspicion she was older.

There were obvious reasons why I didn't want to talk physics. But by the time the edge of hunger had been assuaged, the girl's demands to hear about the nature of electric charge had a curiously commanding ring. So there was nothing to be done except to let the conversation swing to technicalities, away from the matters that were on my mind.

I drew pictures and jotted down various equations on the back of a menu. When I was through all the explanations, she said, "You'll get a fair measure of success with that approach, but it's very ugly."

"Can you suggest one better?"

"Yes, of course, but not without quite extensive changes. The whole way of writing the theory needs inverting. Instead of using space-time for the basic variables, put field quantities as the independent variables in the equations that describe the particles."

"Which is something I've vaguely wondered about—getting space-time as a derived quantity, getting it from field variables with a degree of arbitrariness equivalent to the usual invariance conditions."

"Well, you'd better stop vaguely wondering. I'll show you later how to get started, although I really oughtn't to be telling you all this."

The waiter brought the dessert. I waited for him to leave before asking the obvious question: "And why shouldn't you be telling me this?"

She answered in a quiet voice, "Because according to what I'm told you happen to be a most desperate and dangerous fellow." Then she laughed quite unaffectedly.

"You must have been told a whole lot of nonsense."

"Oh, I don't think so. About a month ago I read through quite a long and entertaining dossier about you."

Again she laughed, and like a fool I couldn't see the joke.

"When you came here to Ireland, what was it you were looking for, Mr. Fisherman?"

"Maybe you."

"Well, and now you've found me, what do you propose to do?"

"Find out about those equations, of course."

"You don't like being laughed at, do you? You're every bit as bad as the others."

"Did you have a hand in that business on the cliffs of Inishtooskert, by the way?"

This stopped the laughter.

"No, I didn't know anything about it at the time. That particularly futile brain storm was cooked up by Arthur or by his wife. But I did make sure that nothing of the sort was tried again."

"For which my thanks! The blonde climber was Mitchell's wife?"

"Is; the tense is wrong."

"He's welcome to her, the . . ."

"Tsh-sh."

"And what was so futile about the idea of leaving me hanging onto that damned cliff?"

"It was obvious you'd get down. And if you didn't you didn't deserve to, being taken in by a ninny like that!"

"When you've need of it you seem to have access to a pretty fair fund of irrationality, don't you?"

"Look, I think we'd better get back to the car. I dislike having to cross to the island after dark, although with you there, Mr. Fisherman, I suppose I really shouldn't worry. You'd better pay the bill. You do pay the bill, don't you?"

"Yes, I pay my debts."

"That's rather what I thought. I do too."

The girl drove the car rapidly northward toward Killorglin.

"I suppose you know that the northern peninsula is out of bounds for me?"

"Scared? Do you want to get out?"

"The answer to both questions is no. I mention it because I shall have to depend on you to get me through the security checks."

"Do you suppose the thought hadn't occurred to me?"

"A while back you mentioned a dossier. Have you any idea where the information in it came from?"

"If I wanted to be unkind, to baffle you, to keep you quiet for a few minutes while I concentrate on driving this car, I'd tell you that Seamus Colquhoun happens to be one of our best agents—we have some, you know. Does the name mean anything to you? I think I've got it right."

Here was a minor mystery cleared up. Now I knew how Mr. John Chance had got hold of Parsonage's passwords, and with this knowledge I remembered exactly where I'd seen Mr. Chance for the first time. And now I even understood the motive for his visit to my cottage.

It boiled up inside me: not anger, but helpless laughter.

"So you have a sense of humor after all!"

"Then it was pretty well a miracle that I got anywhere at all."

"It was utterly astonishing. We never reckoned that anybody would have the hardihood—or should I say the fool-hardihood—to bring in a boat on a night like the one on which you came to Inishvickillane. You see why I said it was ridiculous to think that you could be finished off with that cliff trick. When someone shows himself to have the luck of the devil, a sensible person draws the obvious conclusion."

"How did you come to get hold of the dossier?"

"I suppose I'd better explain a few things. I never intended to leave you kicking your heels around Caragh for so long. But for some months I was terribly busy, and by the time I got round to it our people had made a silly sort of game out of teasing you."

"Would you call making me lose my memory a piece of teasing?"

"When you come to hear the full story of the memory business, you'll see there were two sides to it. I think you'll agree that you've really made a pretty good bargain."

"And Mr. John Chance?"

"Yes, that was rather well done, wasn't it? But trying to isolate you, to keep you odd man out, wasn't at all sensible. After what had happened already, it was perfectly clear that you'd manage to fit everything together sooner or later. The interest of the game was to see how you'd do it, just where you'd pop up. I could have died of laughter when I saw you in the computer room today. But I'll say no more, or you'll be getting conceited, if you're not that already."

There was no danger of adding to my conceit, for this was one of the most deflating remarks I'd ever heard. If this incredible girl had been laughing at me, how had she been able to correct such a huge difficult program on the computer?

We took the road through Milltown and turned off for Dingle at Castlemaine. There were three security controls at various points, but the girl and the car were apparently well known, for we passed through them almost without stopping.

The clouds flared red in front of us as we left Dingle behind. I think both of us were conscious of chasing the declining sun as we drove up the incline to Ballyferriter. In spite of the matters that were insistently running through my head, it was impossible not to be overwhelmed by the blazing western sky. We stopped the car along the road between Ballyferriter and Dunquin, and climbed away onto the rough moorland. The sea below us was alive with a liquid fire.

Suddenly the girl was shaking with violent, uncontrolled sobs. By now I was inured to most occasions of surprise, but this was utterly beyond expectation. I slipped my arm around her. She tried to shy violently away, but I held fast and soon she stopped protesting.

We returned to the car and I took it the last part of the journey to Dunquin Harbor. Because of the ideas that danced in my head I found the driving horribly difficult, for the incredible solution to the main mystery had suddenly leaped into the glaring light of consciousness.

17

INISHVICKILLANE AGAIN

The light was fading quickly as we moved out from Dunquin, headed south of Blasket. There was much on my mind, above all there was much that I wanted to ask this strange girl. But this wasn't the right time or place, what with the noise of the engine and the sound of the sea slapping hard on the boatside.

Besides, I was still half unnerved by the deception of Seamus Colquhoun. Not that this was a matter of much importance any longer. But what a fool I had been to be taken in by the wretched man! True, I had always felt somewhat uneasy in my talks with him, but this very agitation had somehow contrived to mislead me. The amazing thing was that he had never tried to find out who had sent me, or anything about my mission—he didn't even seem to know my name. If he had ever shown the least curiosity my suspicions would probably have been roused—at least I hoped so.

Then in a further flash I saw the reason. Because anything I could have told Colquhoun was already known to I.C.E. How, and from where, I still couldn't say. Percy Parsonage? I doubted it—I simply had to doubt it, otherwise my reason must have given way. Mr. Rafferty? I doubted this too. Rafferty wasn't in the right class. But then, if I'd misjudged Colquhoun, why not George Rafferty too? No, no, this was beyond possibility.

Then I saw the whole business as it must have seemed to I.C.E. First, the fantastic business on the train to Fishguard. Papa Percy's blood had got me into Ireland all right, but not at all for the reason he expected. Who would have had the heart to keep me out after that affair? How they must have laughed! But I suspect the homeric aspects of the matter probably wore a bit thin during my first week in Dublin. My small-minded antics, in museums, at 18, St. Stephen's Green, with Sam Lover and Buck Whaley, were not at all to be favorably compared with the robuster concepts of the ticket collector, Karl, Inspector Harwood and the imaginary body.

As I say, I think I.C.E. lost patience after that tame first week. I think they decided to pull me in as soon as I appeared at Marrowbone Lane. And not to be outdone by Parsonage's affray in the train, I think they put on a similar ribald show, with Liam and the Irish stage character, and with the posse of police. But for the first time I won a few points in the game; I wriggled out of the net, in a way that could hardly have been guessed beforehand.

After that, I was manifestly given a fair amount of rope. And why not, since Colquhoun must have known about Houseman and P.S.D.? He must have known that in sending me to Longford he was playing a master stroke.

Yet from the moment I stepped off the bus at Tang the game swung more and more in my favor. I think they lost my track as I walked my quiet gentle way through the lanes and fields of Ireland. I think the appallingly unlucky coincidence at Slievenaman with its ghastly outcome was more than they bargained for. I think they only picked up the trail again at Shannon Airport, almost certainly because of my booking of the flight to London. No wonder Seamus Colquhoun was waiting there on the road to Kilkee!

This raised another of my failures. The voltage regulator on Colquhoun's car had definitely been wrong—a delightful subtlety on his part, not a chance coincidence as I had supposed. In fact I ought to have deduced Colquhoun's duplicity from this one incident alone. Obviously the true canon had been questioned, and had given the purchase of a voltage regulator as my reason for visiting Limerick.

Yet the lucky shipwreck on Inishvickillane won a major victory for me—I knew it even at the time. But my one moment of supreme triumph was quite missed, the moment in which I had blandly announced my name. This must have come on them like a bolt from heaven. I remembered now the silence of that moment, and I knew that if I had hit hard in exactly the right direction, all could have been settled within the space of a single hour. Instead, I had told a pettifogging, feeble story. After the brilliance of my topological intervention, this must have been an appalling anticlimax. It explained Fanny's sarcastic laughter, and it allowed Mr. John Chance to regain the initiative.

The mere thought of Mr. Chance filled me with a deep shame. Oh, it was so easy to make excuses in plenty: that I had seen him only once before for an odd hour in a poorish light, that I was suffering from a loss of memory, that the bandage on his head made an excellent disguise, that his voice was brilliantly changed. But back in Parsonage's office I had read a dossier on Arthur Mitchell. I knew perfectly well that he was born in Devon, at Barnstaple in 1925. I knew that he won a scholarship to Winchester, which meant that he would have an accented and an unaccented voice both readily at his command.

The boat was approaching the little harbor on the island. In a few minutes I should probably be seeing Arthur Mitchell again. I resolved that on this third occasion the honors of the encounter should be divided a little more equally between us. I would have been quite aghast to learn the margin by which I was to lose this third exchange, for I had still to learn that there is no better way to suppress serious argument than by the popping of champagne corks.

Now we had reached the anchorage. We made fast, climbed the little cliff and started along the path to the stone house.

"And have you got everything sorted out, Mr. Fisherman?"

"Not quite, but I'm making some progress."

"You're an odd fellow."

"Are you thinking of any particular one of my oddities?"

"There aren't many people who know anything about us, but those that do, when they first find out . . ." She paused in mid-sentence.

"Recoil?"

"Not so much physically as mentally."

"And I didn't?"

"No."

"Was it because you thought I might that you never tried to seek me out?"

She took me by the arm. "Look, my fisherman friend, it's nice that you're very intelligent, but there is no need to be quite so clear-headed."

"They" were waiting for us: Mitchell and his wife Harriet, Hertzbrun and the other half-blonde girl—her partner apparently was away. It was interesting that our coming must have been advertised, either by the restaurant or by one of the security controls.

The girl Fanny had evidently entirely recovered herself. She introduced me with obvious relish.

"Arthur, meet Mr. Sherwood. Two old Cambridge men together. You'll be able to have quite a talk."

"I hope the knee is better," I said.

"Very much better, thank you. Did Fanny tell you?"

"No, he guessed all by himself. And here is Harriet, Arthur's wife. But of course you're old friends, aren't you?" The two girls stood side by side, of about the same height with hair of nearly the same color, one with light skin and the other with dark, one with blue-violet eyes and the other with green—a couple of cats watching each other.

"Homer Hertzbrun—Mr. Sherwood. Homer, you should

hear what Mr. Sherwood has to say about the geometry of electric charge."

Then she turned to the other half-blonde, "And now meet my twin—Mr. Sherwood—Mary Ann."

"Well, Fanny, so you decided to get him after all."

"Do you have to sound so predatory?"

"I'm not predatory, I'm just delighted that we shall be able to have some peace now."

It would have been easy to be misled by this innocent conversation. I'd again been astonished by Mitchell's youthful appearance. He certainly looks no more than thirty, I thought; yet the man must be approaching forty-five. There was just one possible explanation. These people must have solved the very difficult biochemical problem of arresting the aging process.

Strange that the old legend should describe the Land of Youth as an island off the Kerry coast. Suddenly I realized what Fanny had meant by the other half of the bargain, and I knew at last just what it was that I felt to be different.

Hertzbrun quickly produced a tray with drinks and glasses.

"That's exactly what I need, Homer," exclaimed Mitchell, "I'm going to drink to the end of my responsibilities."

"I don't get it."

"Of course you get it. I'm going to put my feet up, I'm going to get rid of my ulcers, I'm going to have one long glorious holiday. Homer, my boy, pour me a large tot, a very large one."

"But . . ."

"No buts. It's perfectly obvious. Here's young Sherwood, twenty years younger than me in actual years, and as strong as a horse. Why shouldn't I let him do the worrying? He knows almost as much about science as I do, and he's much more ruthless; in fact he's quite an ugly customer."

"If I might offer an opinion . . ." I started.

"You may not. Yes, much more ruthless. Besides, he's got Fanny's ear, and I haven't. The next phase of development depends on Fanny, and the two of us have too many rows."

Mary Ann laughed, and another small mystery was cleared

away. This was the laugh I had heard over the telephone, on the morning after the visit of Mr. Chance.

"Poor Arthur, if you think they're not going to have plenty of rows you're very much mistaken. Either there will be some splendid rows or Fanny will simply gobble him up."

"Now look here, you're all taking too much for granted, especially Mitchell," I objected.

"It may seem very precipitate to you, Sherwood, but it isn't really. I wonder if you've any idea what it means to start an organization like this absolutely from scratch, to build everything step by step. It's like bringing up a child. At first you think all your worries'll be over in a year or two, but they're not. Then you think everything will be plain sailing after ten years, but it isn't. Then you realize you'll never be out of trouble, however long you go on."

"Stop wailing," said Mary Ann. "Some women bring up six children."

"I'm not wailing. I'm showing Sherwood why it's been on my mind for some time to find someone who could take over the responsibilities. I've had my eye on Sherwood right from the start, or at any rate from the time he finished off those absurd P.S.D. people."

"Right from the start? So you have agents in London?"

"Why be so naïve? Of course we have agents in London. Is that very surprising?"

"It would relieve my mind a great deal to know who it was in particular that forwarded the information about me."

"I don't know that I ought to gratify your morbid curiosity. But you may take it that we knew all about you several days before you left London."

"It wouldn't have been Parsonage by any chance?"

"Oh, no, not Papa Percy. He's a regular fire-eater, the poor old fellow. I had a lot of trouble with him, until I managed to place a very capable girl in his office, one whom you were kind enough to take out to dinner, I believe."

I moaned out loud.

"Are you feeling all right?" asked Mary Ann.

"Hands off! Or you'll get . . ." began Fanny.

"In heaven's name, will you two stop it. Cat and dog, always cat and dog," exclaimed the green-eyed Harriet.

"Now I wonder which is the cat," answered Mary Ann, displaying a full set of teeth.

"Ladies!" exclaimed Hertzbrun.

"You should say 'fair ladies,'" I remarked absently.

"Of course he should," nodded Mary Ann. "Why don't you say 'fair ladies,' Homer?"

"When the wind blows never ask it to stop. Just let it blow itself out," groaned Fanny.

"How did you find out about the petrol bombs?"

"Oh, after we got our first report, from one of our men— a Seamus Colquhoun if you're interested—we sent in our experts. I think they pieced together what had happened pretty well. Incidentally, why did you use two bombs? Wouldn't one have been sufficient?"

"I used two because I'm an ugly customer."

"Which is rather what we thought. Well, as I was saying, I became very interested in you at this stage, particularly when you got away from our frontier patrol in the Boggeragh Mountains. I still can't see how the devil you managed to do that, or how you split the skull of a man seven stones heavier than yourself."

Mitchell began to laugh.

"Look at him, Homer! Sitting there as large as life, imagining himself to be a placid, docile, law-abiding young man." Then he went on with a rush, plainly to stop the irrepressible Mary Ann. "Of course I expected you'd be caught trying to get into Kerry. We put out special alerts to all our patrols. I was flabbergasted when you did get in, and to Inishvickillane of all places."

"Couldn't you have kept a watch on me at Kilkee? Then you must have known that I'd try from the sea."

"We expected you to try from the sea. But we never contemplated either that you'd come in on such a wild night, or that you'd be mad enough to risk this part of the coast."

He paused for a drink. "When you appeared out of the sea, and told such a convincing story with the aplomb of a bishop, I realized that you were probably my man."

"So you promptly arranged to have me killed on the cliffs of Inishtooskert?"

"I must admit that we were a little at cross-purposes over that business. But it was no serious matter."

"No serious matter!"

"Of course not. If you hadn't had the determination to get down that damned cliff, you certainly wouldn't have been our man."

"And if I'd ended by falling into the sea?"

"Well, even more certainly you wouldn't have been our man, would you now, my dear fellow?"

"Didn't I overhear you say something just now about *me* being ruthless?"

"I said you were more ruthless than we are, which I think is true. Look, Sherwood, answer me fair. If you'd tried to kill somebody on those cliffs, would you have given 'em the slightest chance of getting away safely?"

"I'd never try to kill anyone in that way."

"No, you'd feed 'em boron, I suppose—it was boron, wasn't it?"

"I never heard anything about boron," said Hertzbrun.

"Oh, it was just another example of Sherwood's methods. He threatened to feed a boron porridge to one of our doctors —a Dr. Fiddlesticks, or some such name. Then having quite terrified the poor little fellow, he proceeded to cuff him soundly."

"Well, Arthur, I must say I certainly question the wisdom of handing things over to such a bloodthirsty young devil as Sherwood seems to be. Boron and neutrons, eh? A very nasty idea, I must say."

"No, I think you're wrong, Homer. Our policy needs to be more aggressive. Sherwood is just the man to put a real edge on the weapons we've been forging. Look, Sherwood, do you mind if I ask you a straight question?"

"No, no, ask anything. How many pints of my blood did you say you wanted?"

"There's no need to take umbrage, man. What really surprises me is why it took so long—almost a year—for you to get back to Inishvickillane. You see this was a point of some importance to me, because I'd made the decision to carry on until you got back here. I've been getting quite impatient.

In fact I even had to come out and look you up myself, in Ballinskelligs, if I remember rightly."

"I hope I behaved to your satisfaction on that occasion?"

"Entirely so, but really you should have recognized me, you know!"

Then, just as I thought I must burst apart, Fanny laughed and took my arm. "In case you may not have noticed it, he's pulling your leg. You'll have to get used to this appalling madhouse. Let's go for a walk by the sea."

18

AT THE STRAND'S EDGE

The tide was down, so that we could walk the sand by the margin of the sea.

"Don't be misled by Mary Ann. She's really very clever."

"I wasn't misled at all. Was it she who solved the aging problem?"

"You don't miss much, do you? I suppose it was fairly obvious from Arthur. But how did you guess it was Mary Ann?"

"Oh, just bits and fragments of talk, and a good deal of intuition. But that was a very ingenious piece of roughhousing. Did they think it all up while we were driving from Caragh?"

"Most of it, I expect. But you took it very well."

"I took it very stupidly. I just didn't seem to have a single decent card to play."

"Well, it wasn't entirely nonsense. Arthur is very tired, and it has been a long struggle. It's a hard struggle for everybody."

"Why is it so hard?"

"It's hard for Arthur because he's got all the donkey work to do. It's hard for Mary Ann to take anything very seriously. And it's hard for me because I get depressed."

The night was beautifully clear. At last the moment had come to ask the first of the questions that were thundering in my head.

"Can we see it from here?" I said.

The girl pointed to the chain of stars lying between Delta and Omicron Herculis.

"It doesn't seem very much," she whispered, "just a faint thing that you'd scarcely notice without a telescope."

I gazed up at the sky. So this was where it had come from, this bolt of knowledge, this bolt that was going to turn our little human world head over heels. Small wonder I hadn't thought of it before.

"What was the trouble? Increasing heat?"

"Yes, we were slowly cooked alive as our star became brighter and brighter. As generation followed generation, we adapted ourselves as best we could. We lived in vast refrigerators, but in the end nothing could keep out the fierce blast. The rocks became fluid with a liquid fire—it was like the sea tonight when we got out of the car. That's why I was so upset. What is beautiful here was extermination for us. Our planet was wiped clean. An evolution that had taken a thousand million years to develop suddenly ceased to exist."

Once again I slipped an arm around her. This time she laughed. "You wouldn't be doing that if you knew what I once looked like. Not at all like a human."

Now I saw the point more clearly. It would be futile to send a physical body hurtling across space. The essential thing was to send the information, the bolt of information. This would be much easier to do in any case.

"So you changed your body—the chemical part of you, but the electronic side is the same. In computer language, your old brain program was written onto a human brain."

"It was rather like taking a program from a very large computer and attempting to write it into a small computer, like trying to pour a large volume of precious liquid into a tiny vessel—great quantities spilled and wasted. Imagine trying to compress your own degree of perception into the brain of a dog. Everything becomes dim and vague, like a clear landscape suddenly enshrouded in mist.

"After all, we were beings of somewhere between the third and fourth orders."

"Sorry, I don't understand the third and fourth orders," I said.

"Oh, just a rough measure of intelligence. We could handle problems needing somewhere between a thousand million and ten thousand million units of information. Now I'm reduced maybe to around a hundred million."

"Divide units of information by a million and take the logarithm to base ten, eh?"

Fanny very quickly stamped hard on my toes. "Stop talking like a child."

"You've got a lot of power in that darned leg of yours. How did you come by it? I mean were you assembled from raw materials—water, ordinary carbon and nitrogen and so forth?"

"I'm pretty sure not. To construct a human directly from inorganic materials is a problem of the fourth order, and this I think would have been too difficult. It would be much simpler to get the bodies produced in the ordinary way and then to write the information on the brain. I'd guess this to be no more than a third-order problem, if as much as that. But you'd do better to ask Dickey. You haven't really met him yet, but it's much more in his line. You see, the three of us are pretty complementary to each other—Mary Ann and Dickey got the chemical and biological knowledge, while I got the physical. Obviously it's better like this than if we'd all been the same."

"So in the early chemical days of I.C.E. it was the others who supplied the main drive, while now you're responsible for all the new physical development."

"You may say that if you wish."

"So if I were to dump you in the water my job as an agent would really be finished, wouldn't it? Remember what you said about me being a dangerous fellow."

I just managed to get my other foot out of the way in time.

"You don't like being laughed at, do you?—as bad as the others."

"I don't like being taken for a fool."

"Stop being so appallingly human," I said.

She laughed loud and clear above the noise of the sea.

As we walked slowly arm in arm the thoughts chased themselves in my head. Before the moment of extinction arrived, a dying race had somehow managed to transfer a little of its experience and knowledge to another planet. So much was clear. But how had it been done?

The transmission of information from a planet moving around one star to a planet moving around a quite different star was clearly not out of the question. It probably wasn't very much beyond our own present-day techniques. This girl Fanny was manifestly an ordinary human on whose brain the information from another race had somehow been written.

A baby isn't born with a knowledge of physics and mathematics. This comes to be impressed on the brain as the baby grows up: from reading books, from listening to the words of one's teachers—and of course from observing the world around us. In some way I still didn't understand, this normal process had been replaced by a more powerful method, a method controlled by an alien race. The motive of this race was clear—to pass on some memory of itself, to avoid a complete oblivion.

The waves were falling gently on the sand. We stopped for a moment to watch.

"It's very beautiful here. You know, I don't think we had much idea about beauty—there wasn't much of it in our world, I suppose; just a blazing, glaring slag heap."

She kicked a stone into the water. "We weren't angry, just resigned to passing on what we could. But now in some queer way I seem less resigned. What's the point of it all? It'll be just the same here. The earth is already halfway along exactly the same road to extinction. The sun will get inexorably brighter as the years roll by, just as our star did, and life on the earth will just as surely come to an end."

"I suppose that some reasonably sensible game is being played, all right, if only we were clever enough to see it," I said.

"But how clever? It's the lack of detailed balancing that really astonished me—the universe has an enormous effect on us, but we seem to have no reverse effect on the universe."

"I think we might have if only we knew enough."

"To see the complete logical design?"

"To see a logical design better than the actual one. Then I think that something might happen."

"Which may well be true. But we know nothing of the level of intelligence that would be needed," Fanny said.

"Except that humans fall far short of it. Your race fell short, perhaps by a little, perhaps by a lot. It may come at what you would call the fourth order, or at the tenth order, or at the millionth order."

"And I suppose that if a species doesn't get far enough ahead it's simply wiped out, as we were wiped out."

"You weren't wiped out. What you've now got in your head survived. It may save humanity a century, or a millennium. It gives us a push onward down a long road. In our turn we may get nowhere. We may have to end by passing what scraps of information we can to some other creature. But maybe in the end someone will succeed where all the rest have failed."

"All right, Mr. Fisherman, I understand the lesson. It's only when I'm depressed that I become stupid."

We made our way up from the strand. It is a narrow way up the cliffs, but somehow we managed to climb the path, together.

EPILOGUE

The Cointreau was finished, the reading was done, the coffee cold, the fire out, but Geoffrey Holtum sat on, scratching his head.

A 30